# CURSE OF FANGS

## AN IAN DEX SUPERNATURAL THRILLER NOVEL, #6

### JOHN P. LOGSDON
### CHRISTOPHER P. YOUNG

**Published by**: Crimson Myth Press (www.CrimsonMyth.com)

**Cover art:** Jake Logsdon (www.JakeLogsdon.com)

**Thanks to TEAM ASS!**

*Advanced Story Squad*

This is the first line of readers of the series. Their job is to help me keep things in check and also to make sure I'm not doing anything way off base in the various story locations!

(listed in alphabetical order by first name)

Adam Saunders-Pederick
Bennah Phelps
Debbie Tily
Hal Bass
Helen Saunders-Pederick
Jamie Gray
Jan Gray
John Debnam
Larry Diaz Tushman
Marie McCraney
Mike Helas
Natalie Fallon
Noah Sturdevant
Paulette Kilgore
Penny Campbell-Myhill
Sandy Lloyd
Scott Reid
Tehrene Hart

## Thanks to Team DAMN
*Demented And Magnificently Naughty*

This crew is the second line of readers who get the final draft of the story, report any issues they find, and do their best to inflate my fragile ego.

(listed in alphabetical order by first name)

Adam Goldstein, Amy Robertson, Barbara Henninger, Beth Adams, Bonnie Dale Keck, Brandy Dalton, Carolyn Fielding, Carolyn Jean Evans, Charlotte Webby, Dan Sippel, David Botell, Denise King, Helen Day, Ian Nick Tarry, Jacky Oxley, Jim Stoltz, Jodie Stackowiak, Kathleen Portig, Kevin Frost, Laura Stoddart, Lindsay Stroven, Mark Brown, Mary Letton, MaryAnn Sims, Megan McBrien, Megan Thigpen, Myles Mary Cohen, Patricia Wellfare, Ruth Nield.

# CHAPTER 1

One of the things I loved most about living in Las Vegas was the ability to find food day or night. I don't just mean fast food, either. I'm talking pretty much anything you want.

Rachel Cress, my longtime partner at the Las Vegas Paranormal Police Department (PPD) and my girlfriend for the second time in seven years, had been going to see the PPD shrink every few days as of late. She claimed Dr. Vernon was really helping her to break through some relationship issues. I hadn't noticed a difference, to be honest, but I wasn't about to say anything to point that out. Rachel was already quite snarky with me. I saw no reason to make it even worse.

I'd just finished up a cup from the Bones Coffee Company, needing a bit of a pick-me-up before heading into the office. Rachel preferred their Chocolate Raspberry Blend, but I was more into their Bourbon Barrel Aged Coffee. It just had that refined smoothness that I liked to believe fit best with my personality. A fella could dream, right?

But I was also pretty hungry. So I headed out of The Martin, the high-rise building on the Strip where my sweet condo was, and took a stroll toward Tommy Rocker's. They made a Big Ass Burrito that had my name on it.

The night air felt great and since Rachel had taken my Aston Martin, I just padded the back way to get to the restaurant.

Just as I was cutting through the little shopping center next to Tommy Rocker's, a fellow in a multicolored outfit approached me.

He was a djinn with pale blue eyes and long dark hair. I would have placed him to be around thirty-five years old, but it was tough to tell since he was covered with ink. I only saw his tattoos because of my ability to see things like that. To a normal, though, he would have just looked like a thirty-something dude who had a flair for wearing loud clothing. The only tats they'd see were ones that were drawn by normals.

While I was a little annoyed to be interrupted, I wasn't surprised that he approached me. There was a branch of the Djinn Ink Club in one of the hidden zones nearby, after all. These clubs were where normals who were in-the-know went to get a mental fix. Supers also used them, but not quite as often. The clubs were perfectly legal and the djinn community had done well to keep to the rules and regulations. There was a time when that hadn't been the case, but over the last twenty years, they'd run a tight ship. Frankly, if all the other supernatural races and factions would only act like the djinn of today, there'd be a hell of a lot more peace in the world...at least as far as supers went.

"Good evening, friend," the dude said in a sales voice that demonstrated practice. "Fine evening, no?"

"Sure is," I said with a quick smile before holding up a hand to stop him from continuing his pitch. "Before you start, let me just say I fully appreciate that you're just trying to get customers, but I'm not someone who can actually be affected by the touch of a djinn." He gave me a once-over. "Yeah, I know it's difficult for you to believe that, and I'm sure you're wondering who I even am." He said nothing. "Right. Well, I'm the chief of the Vegas PPD, and I'm also an amalgamite. Translation: the dream stuff *sounds* sweet, but they don't work on me."

"Ah," he replied with a slow nod. "It could also be that you've simply never had someone of appropriate skill to lead you on the journey."

This happened from time to time. A new djinn came into town who didn't know about me and my history. Therefore, they made the assumption that they were the *one* who could bring my dreams to life in their unique and somewhat disturbing way.

I typically allowed myself to get into a debate with them about this, but tonight I just wanted to eat.

So I rolled up my sleeve a bit, held out my arm, and gave him a go-ahead-and-try-it look.

He grinned and closed his eyes for a moment.

Now, I've seen a lot of things in Vegas, but there was something really cool about watching a djinn's ink move around as they worked their skills. Sometimes there would just be some slight migration and other times the entirety of their ink would flow to a single point. That's what this guy's tattoos did. All of them poured like a river down his face and neck. He was wearing a jacket, so I couldn't see where else it was moving in from, but when he reached out his hand to touch my forearm, it was liquid black…almost like looking into an inkwell.

I felt the same tingling sensation I'd always felt when they tried this on me. I'd been told that the tingling made them believe it was working on me. Sadly, it wasn't. They just wouldn't know it for a minute or so. I kind of felt like a tease, to be honest.

But there was one thing different this time.

My arm burned.

That was new.

It was as if he were holding a lighter under my wrist from about six inches out. Not excruciating or anything, but certainly uncomfortable.

Still, it was obvious that he had no…

I suddenly felt a bit woozy.

That was odd.

Nausea began to build and I could feel myself sweating. Whispering words began to bounce around in my head along with what sounded like wind chimes. I couldn't understand anything that was being said, and the wind-chimes thing was just weird, but clearly something exceedingly discomforting was taking place.

"What the fuck?" I groaned, barely able to talk.

"The end is near, Officer Dex," cackled his ominous voice. I forced open my eyes to see the djinn staring at me with a sinister smile on his face. "It's time for you to die."

Did I know this guy?

No time to find out.

I kicked out as hard as I could in order to dislodge him from me. It was a terrible kick, but it worked. He fell backwards, hitting the ground with a thud as I stumbled forward and fell over, smacking my face on the asphalt.

It hurt a fair bit, but my survival mechanisms were engaged, doing their best to keep me from feeling the pain.

The physical pain, anyway.

My emotional well-being was completely fucked.

Worse, I was starting to see things.

There were shadows moving all around me and paranoia was doing its best to dig in and make me its bitch.

"This isn't happening," I panted as I struggled back to my feet. "It's not possible."

"Oh, but it is," the djinn sneered, jumping back at me and locking on again, sending searing pain into the very core of my being. "You are under my control."

I kicked him again.

He fell again.

Honestly, you'd think he would have seen that coming the second time around.

But it didn't matter. His poison had somehow penetrated my defenses and I was in a world of hurt. My blood felt like it was boiling and I had the intense desire to pass out. But I couldn't. I had to fight through this if I didn't want to end up in a never-ending dream dictated by this dude as he fed on me for a very long time.

So, I did the only thing I could do. I fought.

Too bad I was losing.

I knew this because the shadows that had been swarming around started forming into the body of a vampire. He was about my height and build, but he dressed more like Chuck. Very Matrixesque.

"Hey, dickhead," I slurred, "I don't suppose you have any aspirin on you?"

He stepped directly in front of me and smiled, revealing that his fangs were out in full.

While I was still struggling with what was happening here, it seemed incredibly real. Of course, that *was* the trick of the djinn. It was how they wrapped you around their fingers and siphoned your life away for years and years.

Fortunately for me, I knew how the djinn worked. Unfortunately, it was becoming more and more clear that I had finally succumbed to the game.

Not fun.

Just as the vampire's eyes began to turn red, I held up a wavering hand in warning and grumbled, "Stay back or I swear I'll fall over on you."

He attacked.

# CHAPTER 2

*E*ven in my dazed state, I wasn't someone you wanted to fuck with, unless you had a penchant for being hurt.

The vampire, real or not, was on me like stink on shit. We hit the ground and were rolling around like a couple of dudes in an Ultimate Fighting Championship bout at the Mandalay Bay on fight night, except neither of us was wearing shorts.

He'd brought his fangs toward my neck more than once, but I kept dodging. I wasn't worried about being infected by vampire venom or anything. I was already genetically a bit vampire, though I loathed to admit that, but imagining the joy of having two long-ass pearly whites embedded in my neck was not pleasant.

"Get off me, asshole," I raged through hallucinations, rolling over and lashing out at him with my fist. It was a great punch. One of my best, in fact. Too bad it hit the pavement instead of his face. "Goddammit!" I yelled, clutching my now broken hand.

He kicked out at me, launching me to the side. My head hit the ground again.

This little game of fight-the-vampire was certainly not making me better looking.

It took some effort, but I finally got back to my feet. Blood from my forehead started to drip down into my eye. It stung and made the world blurry.

"Where are you at?" I choked, spinning this way and that, trying to spot him. "Come on, dude. Let's do this."

Honestly, I felt like I had gone on a bender and downed a solid ten Rusty Nails...on an empty stomach. If they were filming an episode of *Drunk History* in town, I'd have been at the top of the list for a guest spot.

"You can't win, Dex," I heard the djinn say from my right. "You're under my control."

That pissed me off.

It was one thing for me to give up control to someone, like a succubus, for example. That was fun and usually had a happy ending, if you see what I mean. Being taken over without my permission, however, was not something I found tolerable. I'm sure I'm not alone in this feeling, but the difference between me and most people was that I fought like a crazed demon when I felt trapped.

So I backhanded the djinn and swung wildly at the vampire, broken hand and all.

The djinn fell down again. He was clearly not very good at fighting. But the vampire ducked my punch and sent an uppercut that made me glad I hadn't had my tongue sticking out. If I had, it'd have been half its current length. That wasn't something I'd want to break to Rachel.

My teeth vibrated as his fist slammed in again, this time driving me to my knees.

This was simply not a fair fight.

"You guys are being real dicks," I wheezed as the vampire connected with another right. "Dude! What the fuck?"

I tried to reach for him, but my mind was simply too far gone.

Bottom line was that I was screwed. This fight was a complete loss. My only hope was that Rachel and the rest of the PPD crew would be able to find me.

That's when I had the thought to use my connector.

Duh.

Sometimes, though, timing was everything.

The instant I went to contact to Lydia for help, the vampire bit into my neck, bringing forth a level of pain that not even a safe word could manage.

"Biscuits," I whimpered, trying anyway.

It didn't work.

Nor did it stop him from unleashing that vampire venom of his into my veins. The world threatened to close down, leaving me in a pit of darkness. My eyes struggled to stay open.

But then clarity began to come back.

It was slow at first, barely a flicker. It still wasn't *me*, exactly, but at least I wasn't sinking into oblivion. The intensity grew and grew until I felt a ferocious focus that required blood to be sated.

JOHN P. LOGSDON & CHRISTOPHER P. YOUNG

With a heave and a roar, I flung the vampire away like he was nothing.

I threw him so far, in fact, that even I was surprised by my strength.

My blood burned and the sounds in my head were threatening to drive me insane. Something in the back of my mind begged me to contact Lydia, but it was like I'd forgotten how.

I was hemorrhaging madness.

My eyes locked in on the djinn.

He was the one who had done this to me. He was the one who had to pay. He was the one who *would* pay.

"Now, wait," he said, putting his hands up as I began to stalk him. Clearly he saw what lay behind my threatening eyes. "Just stay back. I'm your master, remember?"

"Death," was my response, and it didn't even sound much like me. "Death."

The *me* who was still living in my head felt like he was getting smaller and smaller. It was as though I were being taken over by something far more powerful than I could even imagine. I couldn't explain it, nor did I really want to. I just knew I needed to escape it somehow.

But how?

*Antitoxin.*

That was one of those words that Gabe the vampire had fed to me. His mystical no-user-manual words were a thing of legend at this point. He gave me such treats as *Flashes*, which allowed me glimpses into someone's past; *Time*, which was great for watching a woman have a really slow orgasm, and also for slowing time in general; *Sniff*, which had helped me have the scent-tracking capabilities of a wolf; *Words*, which was the one I'd used to battle against a pixie in a *Joke-Off*; and now *Antitoxin*, which I could only hope would heal me from whatever the fuck was going on right now.

"Anusflopsin," I attempted, sounding like a drunken sailor. "Oh, come on!"

"Stay back," screamed the djinn. "I'm warning you."

That wasn't the right thing to say, apparently, because the beast inside of me only took that as a challenge. Contrary to popular belief, using bravado against something that can kill you is only slightly less dumb than using bravado against something that can kill you and really *wants* to kill you.

He raised his hand in defense as I attacked, but there was no use.

My fangs came out and I bit into his neck with reckless abandon, nearly ripping his head clear from his body.

He fell limp as his blood spilled from my lips.

I spun around and saw the vampire who had attacked me. With the djinn being dead, that meant *he* hadn't been a hallucination. I was kind of amazed I was able to deduce that in my current state.

The vampire's face turned white as he stood there staring at the fallen djinn.

Slowly, his eyes came up to meet mine and he looked terrified.

"What happened?" he said, clearly baffled. "Why am I here?"

The beast within me wanted to lunge out and crush the life from him, but there was enough of *me* left to sense that this poor vampire had been duped by the djinn just like me. We were in this nightmare together.

*Antitoxin.*

My breathing was becoming labored, and I sensed this was because I needed to kill again. Obviously, this is what being a frenzied vampire felt like. I don't recommend it.

"You need to run," I warned the guy in the trench coat as my drunken stupor continued to be replaced with pure focus. My voice was hoarse. "I cannot control this for much longer."

*Antitoxin.*

"I didn't know," he stammered, taking a step toward me.

"Run!" I stormed.

He shrieked and then took off, bolting toward Tommy Rocker's.

I had to wrench my gaze away because the chase was incredibly tempting. When I turned, though, I saw the fallen body of the djinn and what I'd done to him. At least I no longer craved that burrito.

"Ew," I said, indicating that there was at least a little of me left inside my quickly deteriorating mind.

*Antito—*

"Yeah, yeah," I grumbled, working hard to focus. I could either think or say these special words as long as I did so intentionally. Out of sheer determination, I stared at an indent in the asphalt and whispered, "Antitoxin."

I convulsed, screamed, and then fell flat on my face.

## CHAPTER 3

*W*hen I finally came to, I had fully healed. That was one of the many nice things about being an amalgamite. I healed fast. That didn't mean I was an immortal or anything. I *could* be killed. The throbbing in my head told me that I nearly just was, in fact.

I did find it a bit strange that nobody had stumbled across me or my djinn buddy. I squinted and found we were in a null zone. Translation: no normals were looking.

"*Lydia,*" I called to our base A.I. as I slowly got back to my feet, "*I just ran into a bit of a struggle down here with a rogue djinn.*"

"*Is everything okay, sweetie?*" she replied in the sweet voice she only used with me.

Everything *wasn't* okay, no, but I wasn't going to tell her that. Saying something would only land me in a meeting with the Directors. I wasn't ready to deal with them just yet.

"*I'm fine*," I replied. "*Please have Portman send someone over to pick up the body. I'll set it in a hidden zone at my location.*"

I heard a tone that told me Lydia had a fix on me.

"*I've put in the request, puddin'.*"

"*Thanks, baby*," I sighed and disconnected.

I was still unclear as to what had just happened. I'd never been in a situation where a djinn was able to do the mental hokey pokey on me. That made me think he was another uber, just like Reese, Shitfaced Fred, and so on. But this guy was *too* easy to kill. If he had been an uber, I doubt that a quick bite…

I paused at the memory of my chomping into his throat. Doing that would have required me to have fangs. Right?

Fuck.

I gingerly reached up and ran a finger along my teeth. They felt the same as always. Nothing pointier than normal, anyway. But I had the sneaking suspicion that if I really wanted them to pop out…

Shit. They did.

"Thon of a bisch," I lisped and then, hearing myself, I added an eye roll. "Great. Tho I have fangth *and* I thound thtupid. How do theth guyth pick up chickth tho eathily?"

I pulled my fangs back in while rolling my eyes once more.

Ugh.

"Okay, Ian," I said to myself as I tried to comprehend everything that had just happened, "you were touched by a djinn who was actually able to mess with your mind, you were bitten by a vampire who was also suckered into this by the djinn, and when that vampire's venom sank into your system, you went seriously fucking ballistic."

So why would the venom do that to me?

The fact was that components of all races had been found in my genetic makeup, including vampire, but this was the first time fangs had ever popped out. Could that mean other things could show up at the surface, too? Was *Ian the Werewolf* in my future? I groaned at the thought, hoping it would *not* be the case. The last thing I needed was to start marking trees in my neighborhood.

I had to figure this shit out.

Seeing that I wasn't hungry anymore, I started heading back to my condo, wondering who I could turn to for help.

There was only one person I could think of who may have answers.

Gabe.

The problem was that he had a tendency of only showing himself after my crew and I finished whipping the crap out of an uber. Or maybe it was after I used his special code words? Maybe both? When we'd defeated Reese, I had no special words. Bah! Who the hell knew what his triggers were? Regardless, I'd already used the *Antitoxin* word he'd given me. If he somehow knew that, maybe it would be enough to bring him out of the shadows.

Honestly, I wished I could just speak with the Directors about this stuff. They were my bosses. They *should* have my back. But they'd become increasingly more tight-lipped as of late. Getting anything from them was nearly impossible.

"*Hey, babe,*" Rachel called through the connector just as I was about to hit the lobby of The Martin, "*I'm back and about to take a shower. You nearby?*"

I didn't want to tell her what had happened until I had more information, or at least until I'd tried to get more information.

"*I was just about to come up,*" I replied, "*but since you're back, I'm going to snag the car and make a quick trip.*"

"*Where are you going?*"

"*Three Angry Wives Pub,*" I replied, knowing she wasn't a fan of my frequenting the place. "*Need to see if Gabe is there.*"

"*Why?*"

"*I was thinking on my walk about things and I need his input,*" I answered somewhat cryptically. "*It's not a big deal. I should be back to pick you up in about an hour.*"

I could sense she wasn't happy with my lack of information, but she let it go. That was good because I wasn't exactly in the mood to discuss it with her. I knew she'd *want* to help, and that was cool, but her first reaction would be to freak out. That wouldn't help the situation.

We disconnected and I made my way to the Aston Martin and drove off.

The pub was about twenty minutes away, off the main Strip. When you spent your time working primarily *on* the Strip, it was nice to have a place to hide out in. Besides, they had good burgers. Not that I was hungry anymore. In fact, the thought of my ripping into that djinn's neck made me so nauseous that it may have served to curb my appetite for days.

I walked in, snagged a booth, ordered a Rusty Nail, and waited.

Gabe walked in before I'd even had the glass half drained.

## CHAPTER 4

*T*here weren't any pleasantries this time. He signaled the waiter and then strolled over and took a seat, staring across at me.

I gave him a look.

"So are you my fairy godfather or something?"

I had to ask.

"No." He smirked.

"Then how do you know when I'll be here?" I challenged. "And how do you know when I've been in a fight?"

He nodded slowly. "It's in my best interest to know, Mr. Dex. Frankly, it's in yours as well."

It wasn't so much the response as the aloof nature with which it was served that made me want to punch him in the head. To be fair, though, I *was* going through a rumble of emotional angst at the moment. Suddenly having fangs when you are notorious for being irritable when people mistake you for a vampire will set you on edge.

"How is it in my best interest, Gabe?"

"Because you don't exactly get help from anyone else, Mr. Dex. Unless that has changed?"

I sniffed.

"Yes," he went on as his drink arrived, "I thought not. Pity, but expected."

He took a few sips of his bourbon and set the glass down with measured control. See, he *was* a vampire. They were all into that prim and proper crap, except when they were feasting like a rabid jackal, of course.

But my anger was bubbling. I was containing it, but it wasn't easy.

"What's the deal, Gabe?" I asked.

"I've already told you that I'm not in a position to give you further information, Mr. Dex."

I wasn't the type who had eyes that smoldered, but my chemistry was in a serious state of flux and I knew if I didn't release some of this steam, the teapot would start to whistle.

Thus, my eyes smoldered.

"Okay, you fuck wart," I seethed, fighting to keep my voice to a low grumble so as not to freak out the rest of the clientele, "I want some goddamn answers. I've just been fooled by a djinn, bitten by a vampire, and *I* can now grow fangs. Where you may enjoy being one of the fanged ones, I don't."

He sat back, looking nonplussed. He was an arrogant bastard. Of course, that just gave me pause. On a conscious level anyway. Underneath my slowly-waning control raged a beast who was ready to pounce.

"First, Mr. Dex," he said without inflection, "I shall request that you keep the name-calling to a minimum."

"Dick spout," I replied.

He paused and shook his head at me. "Secondly, we have been through this already, and you shall not be changing my position on the matter through threats and intimidation."

"Then why are you here, Gabe?" I asked while pounding the table. Some guests looked over and I gave them a fake smile and a wave before turning back to the vampire before me. "Are you planning to give me another fun word to play with? Maybe *Tickle* or *Jump* or…oh, I know! How about *Bite*? I've got the fucking teeth for it now."

The glass of bourbon came back up to meet his lips.

Oh, I just wanted to kill him.

And why shouldn't I?

He was a vampire, and apparently I was too, now. Didn't vampires always jostle for position? Wasn't that the kind of game they…*we* play?

I cursed to myself.

"Worse than fucking mages," I hissed.

"Pardon?"

"Pardon?" I mocked like a child. That only served to piss me off even more. "Look, Gabe, you're either going to tell me what I want to know or I'm going to kick your ass all over this bar."

He tilted his head calmly. "Are you now?"

Okay, that slowed my aggression. I wasn't ready for a relaxed response to my threat, especially not from a vampire. He was supposed to puff out his chest, show his fangs, and get his eyes going all red and glowy. No doubt like my eyes probably appeared at the moment.

"Yes?" I said, inadvertently making it sound like a question.

Damn it.

After another casual sip of his drink, he leaned forward.

"Mr. Dex, there is nothing to be gained by our fighting. Whether or not you can see it at the moment, I have been your only true asset throughout these last many months."

He kept eye contact, which couldn't have been easy. Smoldering eyes, remember?

"Who else has provided you with any tools needed to defeat the ubernaturals you have been facing?" He sniffed derisively. "Have the Directors been helpful?"

"No."

"No, they have not," he affirmed. "In fact, I would assume they've only become more distant with each demand for information you've given them."

He was right, but he knew that, so there was no reason for me to reply.

"And have you threatened to do them physical harm as you have just done to me?"

I thought back on that. Nothing came to mind.

"No," I replied after a moment. "I *did* call EQK names, but he's kind of a titty swizzle."

Gabe winced. "It appears as though your command over vulgarities is still intact, though I doubt that this has anything to do with the *Words* power I had provided before. Surely that's worn off by now."

"It has," I replied, "and don't call me Shirl…" I stopped myself. "Never mind."

He had a point here, though. Why was I starting to use these colorful names? I usually just went with "dickhead" or "asshole" or something like that. The last few slurs I'd used were a little more creative than I was used to.

My jaw hung open.

"Oh, fuck," I whimpered. "Are you saying that I'm not just doing the vampire thing, but I've got a little pixie in me?"

Yes, in hindsight I realize that sounded very wrong.

To his credit, and likely maturity and class, he didn't reply with a giggle. I would have.

Instead, he merely said, "Tell me everything that happened earlier."

I did, and not just the basic fight stuff, either. I laid out the emotions and everything. It felt like I was in a room with Dr. Vernon's brother or something.

When I was finished, he sat back and pulled the glass of bourbon to his lips, drinking it slowly.

"The venom has unlocked some of your unique characteristics," he mused, glancing around the room. Finally, his eyes came back up to meet mine. "You will need to keep yourself in check, Mr. Dex. Be wary of who you share this information with. Trust should be provided with extreme caution."

"Even with you?" I asked pointedly, even though it was clearly too late.

"Again, Mr. Dex, I've been your only true help in all of this." He pushed away from the table and stood up. "Can you say that about anyone else?"

"Yes," I replied without hesitation.

He stopped and furrowed his brow. "Oh?"

"My entire team, Gabe."

"Ah, yes." His smile was weak. "Sorry, I meant someone of power."

What the hell was that supposed to mean?

"Good evening, Mr. Dex," he said, heading out. "There are no more *Words* for you, I'm afraid."

CHAPTER 5

*W*hen I returned home, I found Rachel waiting for me on the couch. She didn't look irritated or anything, but I could sense she wasn't exactly happy about me being cryptic with her earlier.

"Hey, babe," I said, wrestling with whether or not I should tell her what had happened. "How was your meeting with the good doctor?"

"It was fine," she replied, looking me over, clearly noticing how my suit was all messed up. "How's Gabe?"

"He's…Gabe."

I took off my jacket and looked at it. While I healed just fine, my clothes didn't. I really needed to invest in getting one of those magical tailors to hook me up. Yes, I could afford a few thousand of these suits, but that didn't mean it was good financial sense to indulge in such a way.

"So are you going to tell me what's going on or should I just wait for the made-for-TV movie?"

Honestly, I'd prefer she waited for the movie. I mean,

you gotta admit that it'd be pretty cool to have a movie about all the crap that's happened to me. Right?

But looking into her eyes made it quite clear she wasn't planning to wait for production houses, casting directors, and a budget.

I blew out a long breath.

Rachel was my girlfriend. No, she was more than that. She was the closest thing I'd likely ever get to a wife, life partner, soul mate, or whatever the hell people called it these days.

I took a seat next to her.

"Okay," I said slowly, "I'm going to tell you what happened tonight and I don't want you to freak out."

"Why would I freak out?" she asked pointedly.

I told her everything that had happened, except for the bits where I got really emotional. I left that junk out.

"So you're telling me that you're a vampire now?" The question came with a couple of disbelieving eyebrows.

"I knew you wouldn't believe me," I groaned, "and I *really* didn't want to have to do this, but here you go."

My fangs popped out.

Her eyes nearly did, too.

Then a little sinister grin came over her.

"Sexy," she said in a cat-meow sort of way.

"Theriouthly?"

She did a pig-snort laugh in response, quickly covering her mouth.

"Nice lisp."

"Well, it'th not like theth thingth are eathy to…" I trailed off as her laughter broke out in full. The fangs went back in. "I'm incredibly happy you find this funny, babe."

Rachel clearly caught on that she was being ridiculous. This wasn't a joke, after all.

"Shit," she said, instantly recovering. "You're right. I'm sorry." Then she shook her head. "But you've always been partially vampire, so this can't be a huge shock to you. My guess is that you just had some sort of reaction to the vampire venom and it'll pass as soon as your body has time to properly process it."

I hadn't considered that. Gabe didn't point it out as being an option either. Maybe he didn't know? He seemed to know a lot more about me than others did, but that didn't mean he knew *everything*.

"That's actually a good point," I started, but then reality struck. "Wait, no, that's not right."

"Why not?"

"Because, Rachel, I'm also using creative foul language when I'm really riled up."

She squinted and looked up to the left. "So?"

"So that means the pixie components of me have also been unleashed." I held up a hand before she could respond. "No, Rachel, a pixie did not bite me, too."

"Hmmm."

My lady leaned back on the couch and crossed her arms. Usually when she did this, it meant I'd done something wrong, was doing something wrong, or was about to do something wrong. She was known to cross her arms rather frequently around me.

"Does anyone else know?" she finally asked.

"Just Gabe."

"Do you trust him?"

"No," I answered. "I mean...not a lot." I moaned and began rubbing my temples. "Fuck, I don't know. He has been the one feeding me these special skills that have helped us defeat these damn ubers as of late."

"True," she said. "Still, though, you might consider telling the Directors what's going on."

My eyes shot over at her so quickly that she seemed taken aback.

"Not a chance," I said, "and I'm telling you right now not to say anything to anybody about this until I have more information."

She put her hands up in surrender. "Okay, okay. No need to bite my head off."

That brought back the image of what I'd done to that damn djinn. Yes, he'd had it coming, but it still didn't sit well with me. The thought made me sick.

"I'm sorry," I rasped, putting my hand on her knee. "Look, I'm kind of mentally screwed up right now. My hormones are all out of whack, my emotions are completely shot, and I have the intense urge to kill anyone who even *thinks* about fucking with me. Do you have any idea what that's like?"

Her response was in the way of a dull look, followed by, "If you're having cramps, I'll get you some Midol."

I cracked a smile at that.

"Nice."

We sat in silence for a few minutes. Obviously, she was processing things as much as I was. If there was any one person I could count on, though, it was her. The jury was still out on Gabe. I was hopeful, but I'd been around the block too many times to put my cards on the table with him just yet.

"What about the rest of the team?" she asked.

"I'm not sure yet," I answered her sadly. "I *want* to trust them, and I probably will, but for now…no."

Just as I was about to go into my reasoning behind this, my connector went off.

"*Chief,*" said Warren, the PPD wizard, "*you there?*"

"*Hey, Warren,*" I said aloud *and* through the connector as I shrugged at Rachel while patching her in. "*What's up?*"

"*You're not going to believe this,*" he replied, "*but I'm down at New York-New York—*"

"*Why wouldn't I believe that?*" I asked, making an I-think-Warren-has-been-drinking sign at Rachel. "*I'm sure you go to many casinos during your free time.*"

Rachel rolled her eyes.

"*Yeah, okay,*" he said, sounding confused. "*Anyway, I'm calling because there are a bunch of goblins down here wearing pinstriped suits, smoking cigars, and waving tommy guns around.*"

"*Well, that's not good.*"

"*Nope. They haven't done anything yet, but I've got a bad feeling about this.*"

"*Have you already contacted Lydia?*" asked Rachel.

"*Oh, no…I uh…*" He cleared his throat. "*I'll do that now.*"

"*Thanks, Warren,*" I said. "*We'll be right over.*"

I dropped the call and looked at Rachel. She seemed to be just as perplexed as I was. We hadn't seen goblins up in Vegas much over our time together, and we'd *never* spied any of them dressing up as gangsters.

"This should be fun," she said with a look that countered her statement.

"Yeah," I replied, jumping off the couch and running back to my closet to snag a fresh jacket. "I'm sure it'll be a goddamn riot."

CHAPTER 6

It was a quick ride over to the New York-New York casino from The Martin. Parking was easy with the PPD. Throw out a null zone and pull up to the curb. All the normals moved over like there was construction or a broken-down car sitting there. Any supers who were driving moaned and groaned, but eventually got over it.

"I'm feeling irritable," I admitted as we walked through the front entrance and cut right toward the casino. "I may have to take a backseat on this one, Rachel."

"I can run things, if you need me to," she replied, keeping her pace brisk. "It's not like I'm a rookie here."

I sniffed the air and caught scent of Warren.

That was weird.

I'd been given the *Sniff* command from Gabe when I had gone to London, and I remembered how intense the sensation was. This was not quite as strong, but it was damn sure more sensitive than my normal sense of smell. Great, that meant my werewolf side was surfacing.

"We just need to find—" she started, but I grabbed her arm and headed toward the casino. "This way, then?"

I peered at her from the corner of my eye.

"You know, Ian," she said, grinning, "I have to say that I'm a fan of this brooding you're carrying about with you. It's so much sexier than the nice-guy thing you usually do."

My brooding turned to distaste.

"Ew."

"Don't 'ew' me," she huffed, pulling her arm from my grip. "You're the one who likes whips and chains, remember?"

"Uh…"

"Maybe *I* wouldn't mind a little play in that direction from time to time, too, you know?" She seemed serious. "Dr. Vernon thinks it'd be good for us."

I wanted to say "ew" again, but instead went with "Sorry."

We circled the center bar and walked straight up to Warren. He was seated on the opposite side of the entrance, and he was drinking what appeared to be a strawberry daiquiri. I looked at it dubiously and then blinked at him.

"Want some?" he asked, holding it out.

I *did*, especially because the pureed strawberries smelled delicious, but I wasn't going to give in to temptation. I had a reputation to uphold, after all. Besides, another sniff told me there was no alcohol in it.

"No, thanks," I replied with a heavy dose of sarcasm, "I had a juice box on the way over."

"Oh, cool," Warren remarked. "I love those."

"Riiight," I said at length. "Anyway, you…"

I paused and sniffed the air again. There was a scent of cheese and sweat, of finely pressed suits, and of chiseled metal with smoothed cylinders. How I could smell that last bit, I honestly do not know.

But it all came down to one thing: goblins.

My eyes sought out the location of the smell. It was off to my left, which also happened to be the direction that Warren was looking…and pointing.

"They haven't done anything besides cause some minor disturbances," he explained. "Everyone around here thinks it's a show."

"And we're sure it's not?" asked Rachel.

"We would have been notified," I answered for Warren. "Well, we *should* have been notified anyway." I turned back to our wizard. "When you reported it to Lydia, did she run a check?"

"She did," he said between sips. "Said there was nothing going on that she was aware of."

So here we were in the middle of the casino with seven goblins holding tommy guns. I scanned them again. Okay, six of them were holding guns. The last one was probably the boss. He needed no guns. He had a coin in his hand and he was rolling it expertly around in his fingers. It rolled over the top knuckles, slid under for a quick reset, and then bounced across the top again. He was clearly the boss. There was just something about him that screamed 'boss.' Confidence. Deadly confidence. He wouldn't think twice about offing any guy on his squad, and that went double for people *not* on his squad.

"What's the play?" Rachel asked.

"You're going to go and tell them to get the fuck out," I answered coldly and then clenched my teeth. "Sorry."

"Oh, don't be," she cooed. "I'm finding it rather interesting."

Warren stopped sipping and slowly lowered his drink. He was frowning at us.

"What's going on with you guys?" he ventured. "Some new sex thing or something?"

My eyes did that smoldering thing again. "What?" I barked.

He nearly fell off his chair.

"Jeez, Chief! Sorry!"

I shook my head and growled at myself. This was *not* going well. I had to get control of myself, and quick.

"Sorry," I mumbled. "I'm…sorry. It's just that I have—"

"PMS," Rachel interrupted. "He has PMS."

Warren grimaced. "What?"

"Yeah," I concurred, "what?"

"Post Masturbation Syndrome," Rachel clarified quickly. Warren glanced away, appearing confused. Rachel gave me a wink and a thumb's up. "I was away and Ian was alone and…" She leaned in toward Warren. "Well, you know how he is."

Warren edged away from my hands, looking down at them with disgust.

So when I got all angst-ridden and grumpy, Rachel became a goofball? What the fuck was the world coming to?

"*Seriously?*" I said via direct connection. "That's *what you come up with?*"

"*What were* you *going to say, Ian?*" she fought back. "*Maybe something about how the vampire or werewolf in you was aggravated and in need of feeding?*"

"*No, but I wasn't going to tell him that I was feeling surly from jerking off, either.*" I broke the connection and spoke up. "Let's just move on, shall we?"

The goblins pushed the pace before I had a chance to, anyway. Like a small gang from the early twentieth century, they rattled off a number of rounds at the ceiling, causing all the patrons to scream and hit the deck. The only people remaining on their feet when the gunshots stopped were me and Rachel.

We stared at the goblins and they stared at us.

Then their leader gained eye contact with me and smiled.

He had a silver tooth.

# CHAPTER 7

*I* glanced down at Warren and shook my head. I could understand customers hitting the ground, but he was a member of the PPD, for crying out loud.

"*Lydia,*" I called through the connector, "*you're going to need to get The Spin down here for this one.*"

"*I'll let them know, honey cakes.*"

That didn't give us much time before Paula Rose came in and started grumbling at me. Something told me that I wasn't going to be as easy to push around as usual, though. But I *did* feel bad for her this time because there were a lot of tourists lying on the ground here, and things were no doubt about to get worse. That meant she'd have to come up with something good. Unfortunately, the only thing I could imagine that would work was the time-honored "It's a new show that we're trying out in Vegas!" line. Paula hated that line.

Rachel took a step forward and crossed her arms. That

took away the goblin's smirk. Obviously, he had a girlfriend too.

"What's going on here?" Rachel said.

"We's movin' in, that's what," he replied in a New York accent that was fitting for the hotel we were currently in. "This is our joint, now."

"Oh, I see," Rachel replied in mock surprise. "Well, forgive me then. May I ask your name?"

"Spanx."

Rachel snorted and then cleared her throat. "Like the ladies' undergarments?"

"Sure, I like ladies' undergarments," he replied with a shrug. "I don't wear 'em or nothin', but I'm all right with how they look on the dolls."

"Dolls?"

"He's talking like he's from the twenties and thirties," I noted. "They're gangsters, remember?"

"Ah, right." She turned back to the goblin. "Well, it's a pleasure to meet you, Spanx."

He gave Rachel the once-over. "And you is?"

"I'm Officer Rachel Cress from the Las Vegas Paranormal Police Department." She then motioned at me. "This is Ian Dex, he's the chief of our division. And that"—she pointed at the floor—"is our resident wizard. His name is Warren."

Warren waved.

I rolled my eyes.

"So you're coppers, eh?" He grunted and looked at his gang. They chuckled in a not-so-friendly way. "Never much liked coppers, except the dead ones."

"They's best in the grave, boss" agreed another goblin,

"'cause deep down they ain't so bad."

Spanx laughed at that.

"What's your play here, Spanx?" asked Rachel as I casually reached for Boomy. "I'm guessing you don't want to waste a bunch of normals, since that's one of those things that goes on your permanent record."

"You mean what we just done ain't going on our permanent records?"

"Well, uh…," Rachel started. "I mean, sure it will…but, you know what I'm saying."

"Idiot," I whispered and then jolted.

Okay, seriously…what the fuck was going on?

*I* was usually the one saying the stupid shit to the perps, and then *Rachel* called *me* an "idiot." Now, granted, I was also usually the one talking to perps and not Rachel, so maybe this was just validation that I wasn't any more of an idiot than anyone else.

That didn't make me feel much better.

Still, for me to call her an idiot just proved I was changing. Change is good, sure, but not when it happens this rapidly.

I was just glad Rachel turned and glared at me. It made it clear that she wasn't as far gone as me. She *was* all into this new Ian-Dex-and-his-brooding-angst-shit that was going on, though.

"Sorry," I mumbled.

She resumed her talk with Spanx.

"This doesn't have to go poorly, you know?"

"Define 'poorly,' doll," Spanx said. "If you's mean somethin' like my chopper squad here fittin' a few coppers with Chicago Overcoats, I'd be good with that."

Rachel furrowed her brow and looked at me.

"Chicago Overcoats?"

"Coffin," I replied and then shrugged. "You may recall that I rather enjoy watching documentaries."

"Uh-huh." She cleared her throat and turned back. "What's it going to take to resolve this peacefully, Spanx?"

"Hmmm," he mused, tapping his chin as he started walking back and forth in front of his henchmen. "I suppose we could start with a nice bag of ice."

Rachel connected to me directly. "*Ice?*"

"*He means diamonds,*" I explained.

"*Then why not just say that?*" Rachel countered.

"Maybe a couple of dames," Spanx went on. Then he paused and scanned Rachel. "A Sheba like you would do the trick."

"*Sheba?*"

"*An attractive woman.*"

"*Oh!*" She smiled and batted her eyelashes. "*He thinks I'm a Sheba?*"

"*Ugh.*"

I want to point out *again* that *I* was the one who just said "ugh" right there. My fangs were itching to come out, too. So were my claws.

This just wasn't my day.

"While I appreciate your compliment, good sir," Rachel said, blushing, "I'm already spoken for."

She motioned at me.

"Bah," Spanx said, waving a dismissive hand at me, "what's this dewdropper got that I ain't got?"

"The height requirement needed to ride the rollercoaster outside," I suggested.

His eyes grew dark. This didn't bother me at all, seeing that mine had that newfound smoldering capability.

"That a short joke, wise guy?" he challenged.

"Tiny *and* bright," I replied without inflection. "Double-threat guy."

"That's it," Spanx said. "Light 'em up!"

I tackled Rachel an instant before the first rounds flew out of those tommy guns. She'd have been torn to shreds by those damn weapons. Of course I would have been too, but Rachel wasn't thinking at the same speed of violence that I currently was. I was essentially a wrecking ball waiting to be unleashed.

Bullets were shattering glasses and bottles as people screamed and crawled, doing their best to get away.

"Stay down," I yelled at those closest to me.

They stopped.

I brought up Boomy and unleashed a breaker bullet right through the nearest goblin gangster. He flew back, crashing into the shoulder of another goblin who was just enough out of the way not to get hit with the same bullet.

"Stop!" Spanx yelled out, causing his goons to quit firing. The crowd was still in a fit of panic, but even they paused. Spanx glared at me. "You wanna play tough, eh?"

He snapped his fingers and a lot more goblins poured out from the space behind him.

Shit.

Then the little goblin boss did something even worse. Something I couldn't have seen coming, even if I'd had all day to study the situation first.

He cast a fireball.

## CHAPTER 8

*T*he bar erupted in flames, but Rachel was quick to hit it with an ice barrage, cooling it off instantly.

"A mage, eh?" Spanx called out. "That'll make things more interesting."

His hands glowed again, as did Rachel's.

This must have been too much for me, because I felt the pulse of magic flowing through my veins. It was like being in the middle of the desert and seeing a nice, cool pool within diving distance. My body was begging me to let it flow.

I held it in check.

"*Chief,*" called Jasmine through the connector, "*Felicia and I are here. On our way in.*"

"*Where are Chuck and Griff?*" I asked, leveling Boomy. "*We could really use them about now.*"

"*On our way, Chief,*" Chuck answered. "*Be there in ten minutes.*"

*"Not sure we have ten minutes, Chuck."*

I fired and fired. The bullets ripped through goblin after goblin, but even I wasn't fast enough to take on this many of them alone. Rachel's fireball left an instant before Spanx's.

Unfortunately, his was stronger. It obliterated Rachel's fireball and then slammed into her chest, throwing her back against the bar.

"Son of a bitch," she shrieked while patting out the residual flames. This was one of the reasons that mages wore those leather outfits. They were infused with magic that helped protect their flesh. "That hurt."

*"Tell her she's got smokin' hot breasts,"* said The Admiral suddenly.

In case you aren't already aware, The Admiral is my dick, and he sometimes talked to me. It was odd. I know.

*"Not now!"* I mentally scolded him. *"In fact, not ever!"*

*"You're such a me sometimes."*

"Huh?"

*"A dick, genius."*

"Oh, right."

Rachel got back to her feet and sneered at the goblin mage.

"There's more of that to come, doll," Spanx announced, getting his hands going again. Then he glanced over his shoulder. "What are you waitin' for? Fire, you blasted morons!"

I could have just dived over the bar at that point and taken the time to enact *Haste*, but I recognized that Rachel would have been destroyed if I did.

So, I let the magic flow.

And flow it did.

It was almost as if I were nothing but a passenger in my own skull. In fact, it felt almost identical to how it felt whenever *Flashes* was activated. The weird thing was that I *knew* what I was doing…I just didn't know *how* I knew.

My hands came up and fire flew from my fingers like I was a human flamethrower.

Spanx's eyes bulged as he quickly built a shield to help protect what was left of his goons. I'd melted at least ten of them before he'd countered my attack.

"Ian," Rachel whispered, stepping over to me with wide eyes, "what the hell is going on?"

"I told you I was fucked up, Rachel," I roared. "Why won't you listen to me?"

"*We're almost there, guys,*" Jasmine yelled through the connector.

"Drop the magic," Rachel instructed me as she slapped my arm. "Do it now!" I did. "You're only supposed to be able to do basic shit like lights and such."

"Don't you think I know that?" I replied as she cast a shield to counter anything that Spanx might consider doing. "Everything in me is unleashing, Rachel. I *told* you that."

"Okay, okay," she said, her eyes darting around. "I just didn't know it was this bad, and unless you want the entire squad to know about it, you'd better keep it under control."

"Warren," I hissed.

"He's on the other side of the bar, crawling along with the others."

"Unbelievable."

"Yeah," she agreed. "Anyway, what do we do here?"

I pointed Boomy in the direction of Spanx and fired. The bullet fell after smacking his shield. I grunted at him and rolled my eyes.

"We kill them," I seethed. "We kill *all* of them."

## CHAPTER 9

*S*panx clearly saw the look in my eyes that spelled his doom because he pointed his crew to attack us, and then he slipped back into the shadows.

Felicia and Jasmine ran onto the scene the opposite way that Rachel and I had come in.

The rat-a-tat of tommy guns rang out, bouncing off Rachel's shield.

I wanted to light up the area with more magic, but Rachel was right about my having to keep it under wraps for now. I had a feeling that Jasmine sensed something was up with me, though, because she was eyeing me dubiously from her side of the room. Worse than that, Felicia was sniffing in my direction. She'd clearly caught wind of something. I sniffed back, picking up her scent. The werewolf in me was definitely alive, and she was intoxicating.

*"Does this mean we get to play with her again?"* asked The Admiral. *"I always liked playing with her."*

"*Will you* please *shut the hell up?*"

"Who is he talking about?" Rachel said, one eyebrow raised.

I often forgot that Rachel was what I called 'a cock whisperer.' She could hear the conversations between me and The Admiral. As far as I knew, she could only do that with me. Then again, as far as I knew, I was the only person alive who could have conversations with his own manhood. Of course, this meant she'd also heard it when The Admiral made the comment about her chest being on fire.

One sigh later, I answered her.

"Felicia."

She tilted her head.

"She's a werewolf," I pointed out. "I'm not in control of things at the moment, as you know."

"I do," she replied, "but let The Admiral know that if he so much as attempts to play around with Felicia, or anyone on the crew, I'll personally evict the two neighbors that are dangling beneath him."

"*Ouch.*"

Rachel knew I didn't play around with anyone on the crew. Well, except her, but that was only because we'd come to an understanding. But it wouldn't have mattered if Felicia was on the crew or not, I was one of those guys who was fiercely loyal. I didn't cheat. Period.

"All right," I growled at her, "enough with the threats. Regardless of whatever the fuck I'm going through, you know who I am."

She blinked a few times as the flush of red faded from her face.

"You're right. I'm sorry."

I nodded and then opened a broadcast on the connector.

*"Jasmine, cast some energy shots at their guns,"* I commanded. *"I want those weapons on the ground fast."* Her hands started to glow. *"Felicia, sniff out their leader. He's a mage who has no weapons."*

*"Technically,"* corrected Rachel, *"he* is *a weapon."*

A few moments later, little electrical shots flew from Jasmine's fingers, smacking gun after gun. The wielder of each yelped and dropped their weapon. The rest of them spun and started unleashing hell at my mage.

Fortunately, Jasmine had been through many a firefight. She dived to the ground, staying clear of the gunfire. That gave me time to rush the little green fuckers.

I was usually the type of guy who would just shoot you and be done with it, but the torment infusing my psyche was on overdrive.

Thus, I grabbed the first goblin I could, picked him up by the neck with one hand, and punched him so ferociously with the other hand that I thought certain his head was going to pop off. I hit him so hard, in fact, that it killed him due to a snapped neck.

Normally this type of thing would have given me pause.

It didn't.

What it did do was give me an idea.

I dropped the dead goblin backwards, grabbing him by his ankles, and then started swinging him around like he was a golf club. I clubbed into goblin after goblin, yelling "fore!" after each crunching hit. Whether I was killing these guys or just knocking them unconscious, I couldn't say, but there was definitely a fair amount of blood painting the walls.

The goblins I hadn't struck yet turned tail and poured through a hidden zone. I knew this because they disappeared.

I launched their decimated pal in after them.

"*Hidden zone,*" I yelled out as I ran toward it. "*Let's go!*"

Felicia slipped in before I did, making it clear she was hot on the trail of the weaponless-goblin.

My senses jolted at the close scent of her.

I got the feeling that The Admiral wanted to say something, but he wisely decided to keep it to himself for now. He didn't want to tempt the wrath of Rachel, after all. Bottom line was that even if your downstairs neighbors *are* a couple of nuts, you can still find yourself pretty attached to them.

"*Chuck,*" I called out, "*we're going into a hidden zone. You, Griff, and Warren need to work with Paula to get things squared away out here.*"

"*Paula?*" Chuck replied with a whimper. "*Oh, come on, Chief. She's a—*"

"*It's not up for discussion, Chuck,*" I spat back. "*Just do your fucking job.*"

"*Uh...*"

"*Goddammit,*" I groaned an instant later. "*I'm sorry, Chuck. I didn't mean that. There's something going on with me right now that I can't explain. Just please handle Paula.*"

"*You got it, Chief,*" he replied. "*I shouldn't have bitched about it anyway.*"

That was true, but he didn't bitch about things any

more than anyone else did, including me. Nobody liked dealing with Paula because she was a pain in the ass. But we *had* to deal with her, which meant everyone had to suck it up.

Jeez, even *I* wasn't liking me at the moment.

We were barely twenty steps into the hidden zone when the air grew suddenly cold.

It felt seriously wrong.

I couldn't place it, but…

"Felicia!" I screamed aloud as the reality of what was happening struck me. "Stop!"

CHAPTER 10

elicia had hit a frozen mist.

This wasn't like running into a block of ice, but rather like running into a million tiny razor-sharp ice fragments. It didn't just cut you, its purpose was to shred you.

Fortunately for Felicia, the goblin had only built it to affect someone of his own stature. Therefore, the majority of the shards struck against her leather outfit and not her exposed head and neck. Her clothes got nicked up pretty badly, but those could be repaired. Unfortunately for Felicia, it *did* hit her exposed hands, lacerating them so badly that they turned into two pools of blood.

She screamed and I punched her right in the side of her head, knocking her out cold while dragging her away from the ice.

"*Stay back,*" I commanded Rachel via a direct connection before she and Jasmine made it through the zone. "*I'll tell you when it's safe.*"

"*Got it,*" she replied, thankfully not giving me any grief.

I then put my hands on Felicia's arms and closed my eyes. Warmth flowed through me as a field of vibration began to build. I felt my energy draining, but I wasn't about to let that stop me from doing what needed to be done. Even though heat pulsed in my veins, I couldn't stop my teeth from chattering. It was like standing in the windswept Arctic with your pants on fire.

My head began to pound as I opened my eyes and watched Felicia's hands mend. They hadn't been ripped completely off or anything, but they were a bloody mess… until I was done with them anyway. The scene was mesmerizing. Little pieces of her flesh were grafting themselves together in a lattice of healing.

And this was happening because of *me*.

Once her hands were fully healed, I touched the side of her head where I'd punched her. I felt bad about having done that, but I couldn't have let her go into shock and those hands had been incredibly messed up. Within a few seconds, the bruise was gone and her coloring was normal.

She began to stir.

"What happened?" she asked, blinking in confusion. Then she brought her hands up with a look of horror. "Oh…they're fine." Her confused look deepened. "I thought…" She trailed off.

"*It's safe now,*" I said to Rachel.

She and Jasmine came in and found me helping Felicia off the ground.

"What happened?" asked Jasmine.

"Yes, Ian," Rachel said in accusation. "What *did* happen?"

I gave her a stern look. Then I pointed straight ahead and said, "Frozen mist."

Rachel winced and dropped her head forward. Obviously she got that she was *again* being an asshole. She cursed to herself.

"You're kidding," hissed Jasmine, staring at the mist with wide eyes. "There's a goblin mage with the ability to do that?"

"Wait a minute," said Felicia. "I *did* run into that mist…right?"

"You were close," I lied. "Just as you were about to hit it, I knocked you out of the way. You landed on the ground pretty hard and passed out."

"Oh." She swallowed and blinked a few times. "Uh… thanks, Chief."

"Don't mention it."

I motioned toward the frozen mist and waited for Rachel and Jasmine to dismantle it. That process took them a little over a minute. I had the feeling I could have done it in half the time.

"Let's not move too fast from here on out," I remarked to my officers. "We don't want to run into any more of Spanx's spells, especially since we're all clearly shocked to learn the level of skills he's truly got."

"Agreed," said Rachel. "I'll take point."

We moved as a single unit, going from room to room on this side area of the hotel.

It was one of the sections that all hotels in Vegas set

aside for supers. Actually, you could find these zones pretty much everywhere in the world.

Most of the time they were occupied, though.

This place was barren.

That made me worry.

I had Boomy out and ready, though he honestly felt kind of useless compared to the flamethrower fingers thing I was sporting earlier.

"*Are you okay?*" Rachel asked via a direct connection.

"*I'm teetering on the edge, babe,*" I confessed. "*The amount of power I'm feeling is ridiculous. I honestly believe that I could just have you all go back to the office and kick your feet up while I singlehandedly stop crime in Vegas. And I mean* all *the crime in Vegas.*"

"*Right,*" she said, keeping her voice calm, which was helping me to relax. "*Just remember that this is all very new to you, Ian. You have to take control of it before it takes control of you.*"

"*Feels like I'm already on the losing end of that equation, I'm afraid.*"

And it did.

If you've ever had a taste of power, you know what I'm talking about. But now multiply that by every instance of power you've ever felt and you'll start to understand the breadth of what I was experiencing.

Put it this way, intoxication was too tame a word for it.

But I wasn't stupid. I knew how power worked. It starts small, teasing you. Then you get a little more. Then you want a lot more. The proverbial snowball starts rolling, growing bigger and bigger until it's so large that you can't imagine anything stopping you. You feel invincible. But when something *does* stop you—and it inevitably will—it's excruciating.

*"Hang in there,"* Rachel said. *"Once we get these guys taken care of, I'll give you a crash course in managing your magic."*

*"And what about my fangs and desire to mark everything in the area?"* I challenged. *"And let's not forget my sudden penchant for name-calling, either."*

I grunted at the realization that I'd not unleashed a torrent of names at Spanx. My guess was that I was simply too wrapped up in magic to do so.

Wait.

Maybe that was the key to all of this? Balance?

It made sense, actually. When magic flowed, my fangs *also* stayed in.

This was good information, assuming I was right.

We walked past an opening, when I sensed something wrong again. It wasn't a spell this time, though. It was as if a mass of tiny minds decided it was time to end me.

"Goblins," yelled Felicia as she cannoned into Jasmine and Rachel, driving them to the ground.

I dived in the opposite direction and rolled up to fire Boomy into another shield.

They turned their guns at me and smiled in unison.

My eyes did the smoldering thing in response.

"That's it, you little green motherfuckers," I bellowed like a crazed hyena, "it's blood time!"

CHAPTER 11

$\mathcal{A}$t the rate I was moving, I had the feeling that using my *Haste* skill would probably have felt slow in comparison.

I kicked, punched, snapped, and every other violent word you could imagine as I tore through these guys. They had no chance. It was as though demons had possessed me, bringing along their pissed-off attitudes as luggage.

Bullets were flying from tommy guns and *should* have struck me more than once, but I was just too damn quick. No, I don't mean I was faster than a speeding bullet. I wasn't wearing a cape or anything. What I mean is that I was dodging gun barrels, staying just off to the side of automatic gunfire. As I decimated the goblins ranks, the dodging got easier and easier.

And then Spanx decided to hit me with an energy pulse.

I hated those.

They hurt so damn bad that I often curled up in the fetal position and whimpered like a baby.

Not this time.

This time I growled and launched myself at him.

He shrieked as I got my hands on his neck.

"*Ian, no!*" yelled Rachel through the connector. "*We need him to help us figure out what the hell is going on here.*"

I snarled and lightly head-butted the goblin. His eyes rolled up into his head and all of his goons started yelling, "We give up!" Their guns hit the floor as my crew rushed in and magically cuffed them all.

"*Griff,*" I said through a broadcasted connection, "*we have everything under control in here. How is it going out there?*"

"*I shall answer that by stating that Ms. Rose has arrived,*" he replied in his posh voice. "*She is not pleased.*"

"*Is she ever?*" The question was rhetorical. "*Well, just do the best you can.*" I then patched in to base. "*Lydia, I'm guessing you already have Portman on the way?*"

"*He should be there already, lover,*" she answered. "*Is everyone okay?*"

"*Everyone but the goblins, yes.*"

"*Ah.*"

We disconnected and I turned to Felicia. I needed her to get out of the room. Now. Whatever was going on between her pheromones and my werewolfness was not going to fly. Until I got things sorted out, we had to be kept separated. It was abundantly clear from the look in her eyes that she felt the same way.

"Can you handle Portman and his crew, please?" I asked her.

She gave me a quick nod and split.

"Is there something going on, Chief?" Jasmine asked as she peered up at me from her position cuffing the goblins. "You seem…different."

"Rough morning, is all," Rachel interjected. "We had another fight because he's a big idiot."

We hadn't had a fight, obviously, but Rachel's claim would hopefully prove to distract Jasmine for a while.

"Ah," she said, not looking all that convinced. "I see."

*"Felicia knows,"* I said via direct connection to Rachel. *"She* has *to."*

*"Then you may have to bring her in on it,"* Rachel said, keeping her head down. *"Just swear her to secrecy."*

I nodded to myself, seeing that neither of them was looking at me.

*"I also need to be kept away from Chuck,"* I noted. *"He'll sense the vampire. Shit...fact is that Jasmine is suspicious, too."*

My adrenaline was through the roof. I hated keeping my team in the dark about things. It was hypocritical. Wasn't I the one giving tons of shit to the Directors right now because they were withholding information from me?

But was that even the same thing?

The information they had could help us defeat ubers… maybe. But what did my sudden influx of powers buy my crew, aside from me being really damn strong? They'd understand why I was being snippy, sure, but that could be easily attested to a hangover or, as Rachel had suggested, a lover's quarrel.

*"I'm going to have to be distant until I figure this out,*

*Rachel,"* I mumbled. *"It's either that or bring the team in on things."*

She didn't respond. Then again, she didn't need to. What would she have said?

"Ugh," came the moaning voice of Spanx as he began to regain consciousness. "What happened?"

"You lost, you little taint ridge," I said, glad to hear the pixie in me had surfaced. "Half of your goons are dead and the rest of them surrendered."

"Wise guys," he grunted. "Ain't easy gettin' good henchmen these days, pal."

"Don't care," I hissed, grabbing him by his collar. "What I *do* care about is knowing who put you up to this." I shook him. "Spill it before I drain your blood, you ugly little foreskin wrinkle."

His eyes went wide with fear. Then his brow furrowed and he slapped my hands away.

"Foreskin wrinkle?" he huffed. "What the hell'd ya call me that for?"

"Just answer the question, Spunx," I growled.

"The name's Spanx, pal," he growled back, "and I don't know the guy's name."

Ah ha! So there *was* someone who had put Spanx up to this. I had a feeling that a bunch of goblins wouldn't dare take it upon themselves to jump topside for the fun of it, and Spanx had to know that he couldn't have possibly succeeded in taking over a casino.

"What did he look like?" I pressed.

"How the hell do I know?" he answered. "You all look the same to me. Chins, tits, balls, and asses. That's all I see. Sometimes all on the same person!"

"Fine," I said, trying a different angle, "*where* did you meet him?"

"In the shadows, copper," Spanx answered as if it were a dumb question. "We was on the fourth level in the Badlands, like always, when this lady summons me up out of the blue."

"Lady?" I said.

"Yeah. Some wizard dame. She set the connection. The guy with her was the one doing all the wheeling and dealing." He tapped on his silver tooth for a moment. "Said we was all going to get paid some big coin if we did a run on this joint."

"What about your magic?" I asked him.

He eyed me sideways. "What about it?"

"Have you always been a mage?"

"That's kind of a personal question, ain't it?"

I glared.

"Okay, okay," he said, putting his hands up. "Yeah, was born a mage. Not common for my people, I know."

"You seem pretty powerful."

"That was part of the deal," he mused. "Guessing that's gonna be going away along with the cash, though, ain't it?"

"Quite."

I turned to find Rachel and Jasmine standing behind me. Their faces held as much disdain as mine.

Whoever it was we were dealing with was really making life fun for us. First a djinn that could make me hallucinate, next I got infused with vampire venom so that my genetics started to activate, and now we had a goblin mage with boosted powers who was sent up here by some unnamed jizz canary to take over a casino. My assumption was this person was also the guy who'd brought the djinn on board, giving him the promise of stronger powers, too.

"You'll be stripped of your powers and sent to jail," Rachel stated over my shoulder. "I would imagine you'll be locked away for quite some time."

"Perfect," Spanx said, clapping his hands and rubbing them together while holding a big grin. "It'll be good to see the wife and kids again."

## CHAPTER 12

$\mathscr{I}$ purposely avoided Paula and Portman as I made my way out with Rachel by my side. There wasn't much choice for me but to head back to the office. The Directors were going to want to know what had happened.

"What are you going to say?" Rachel asked, breaking the silence as we drove in.

"I'll just tell them what happened with the goblins," I answered. "Not going to say a damn thing about whatever is happening to me."

"Don't you think they'll notice? You'll be seated in front of a mage, a werewolf, a vampire, and a pixie, Ian."

"I've been doing this for a long time, Rachel," I ranted. "I'm well aware of who the Directors are." Damn it. I'd done it again. "Gah! I'm sorry. This sucks and you should just stay away from me for a while."

"For better or worse, remember?"

I gave her a look that included a squint, a furrowed brow, and a grimace.

"We're *not* married, Rachel."

"Obviously, dipshit," she replied, rolling her eyes, "but the rule still applies."

Well, at least she called me a "dipshit" this time instead of fawning all over me for being a douche banana.

"Anyway," I said more gently, "the Directors aren't technically *in* the room with me. They're viewing remotely, so I don't think it'll be the same thing as when I'm physically present with someone."

"I guess that makes sense," she mused. "Just in case, though, I would do my best to channel a fae or a non-tatted djinn."

She had a point, but I wasn't sure if I could channel either of those races. I hadn't come in contact with any of them.

Wait, I also hadn't come in contact with a werewolf and that little genetic gem was flaring. On top of that, I hadn't come in contact with a mage either, unless you considered my boning Rachel *before* the incident with the djinn.

I had to suppose that djinn or fae were active in me somehow, too. But how do you go about bringing out either of those living in your genetic code? And what about werebear? I would have thought it would jump up just like the wolf, but so far I had no desire to eat honey or salmon.

The vampire in my DNA was easy to bring forth because it just required angst. Same with the werewolf and pixie, actually. The mage probably happened because we were attacked by magic.

But a fae? Did I just have to try and look really, really, really good-looking? Maybe I needed to be a trickster? I honestly didn't know the first thing about being overly sneaky. In fact, I was the guy who got the giggles when I knew a secret that Rachel didn't.

I ran my fingers through my hair as I glanced in the mirror, winking at myself.

"What are you doing?" Rachel asked.

"Trying to turn into a fae," I answered after giving my reflection a smoochie. "They think they're hot, so I'm trying to bring up the fae from deep inside."

"First off, you *are* hot," Rachel stated. "Secondly, how did you get the others to surface?"

"I didn't do anything, Rachel. They just...happened."

"Hmmm." She began tapping her chin. I loved it when she did that. It was cute. "Okay, so go for the djinn, then."

"And how, pray tell, would you recommend I do that?"

She had no immediate answer to that question. Nor did I. If it were only as simple as saying "I want to be a djinn now," that would rock the house.

"Whoa," Rachel whispered an instant later. "Look at your neck."

I did.

Tats.

Just thinking "I want to be a djinn" worked?

Unreal.

Rachel reached out and touched me, running her fingers along the lines of my newfound ink.

"That is so hot."

"You're weird," I rebuffed. "This won't work anyway, unless I wear a turtleneck sweater."

"Why not?"

"Because, Rachel," I laughed, "the Directors know I don't have any tattoos on my neck."

"Oh, right."

I refrained from calling her an idiot, but I'd be lying if I didn't admit I sincerely wanted to. She was letting her libido get in the way of duty and that was...exactly what *I* had done on more occasions than I cared to admit.

"I don't suppose you can do the djinn thing with my dreams, can you?"

"Seriously, Rachel?" I grunted. "*That's* what you want to be discussing right now?"

She nodded. "Kind of, yeah."

This honestly wasn't fair. Rachel was always horny, just like any PPD cop—except Warren and Turbo...and probably countless others, now that I think about it. Anyway, Rachel *was* one of the officers who stayed horny all the time. I was the worst of them all, usually. But there was a time and a place for that sort of thing and right now, right here wasn't it.

"*I think we should roll with it, dude,*" The Admiral suggested. "*We could do all sorts of freaky shit with her at the moment.*"

"*Remember that she* can *hear you,*" I pointed out.

"*I know,*" he said back like he was proud of it.

I peered over and found Rachel was almost imperceptibly grinning. Her face was flushed, too. Great. That meant I was going to have to play a game where I went about tweaking with my girlfriend's dreams.

*"Why are you thinking that like it's a bad thing?"*

True.

As long as she was into it *and* I was into it, who should care? I wouldn't do anything she didn't want to do, after all. That wasn't my modus operandi. Besides, I'd make sure she had a safe word.

We continued the rest of the way in silence, but once we turned in to the main area, I opened a broadcast and doled out commands.

*"Listen up, gang. I'm going in to meet with the Directors about the goblins. While I'm in there, I want everyone scouring for information regarding the guy who put the goblins up to this little show."* I gave a quick nod at Rachel. *"Report whatever you find to Rachel. If you need any details about the final encounter I had with the main goblin, Rachel will give it to you. Ian, out."*

Since when did I say "Ian out?" That was just strange.

Thankfully, Rachel didn't say a word about it. She merely got out of the Aston Martin, walked in beside me, gave me a quick peck on the cheek, and then headed toward the conference room.

If nothing else, I knew I could count on her to get the job done. That was good because I needed to keep to my office as much as possible.

After dealing with the Directors, anyway.

## CHAPTER 13

*E*veryone was present and accounted for. Silver, the vampire chief, sat on the left; Zack, the head of the werewolves, was next; then came O, the lead mage; and last, and most definitely least, was the chief of the pixies, EQK.

The last few times we'd met, it hadn't gone so well. I was always tight-lipped and so were they.

There was once a time when these meetings were almost beneficial. They'd ask how things were going, I'd tell them we had a couple of werewolves defiling public property or maybe a fae scalping hockey tickets, and that'd be that. But then the ubers arrived. Once that happened, our dynamic changed a fair bit. Instead of a relatively decent discourse, I'd get grilled on the ubers, get talked down to a lot, and get the runaround whenever I asked for help.

It got worse after I'd defeated Rot the pixie, though.

EQK had freaked out, spouting off about how Rot was

supposed to have been dead. "Killed during the raids," whatever that meant. I never got any further information because the Directors started yelling at each other until O finally cut communications completely, leaving me sitting alone in the room and wondering what the hell was going on.

Since then, we hadn't discussed anything besides the mundane. Of course, there really wasn't much to talk about since Rot's appearance. Without ubers around, things tended to get a bit boring.

"Mr. Dex," said O, taking lead as he always did, "we heard there was a ruckus down at New York-New York. Anything to report?"

I had to keep myself in check here, especially if EQK blurted something out like he usually did. Technically, I *was* allowed to call him names ever since I claimed that it was a cultural thing for me. They'd argued the point, but seeing that I'm the only amalgamite in existence, my "culture" is pretty much self-determined.

Still, I opted to go pedantic.

"Sir," I said robotically, "there were a number of goblins topside, wearing gangster gear from the early twentieth century. They carried tommy guns and they intended to take over the casino. We stopped them and they are now being processed and will be sent to the Tribunal for sentencing."

"Any fatalities?" Zack asked.

"Goblins only, sir."

"How many?"

"Last count was eleven," I answered, thinking it was

probably more like eighteen. "I can have a final tally sent to you once we have completed our paperwork."

The air in the room felt stale to me. Like it was barely moving. This probably had to do with the fact that I didn't like this part of my job, especially since information flow seemed like a one-way street with these guys.

"Were *any* normals affected adversely?" asked Silver in his smooth voice.

"None that I'm aware of, sir," I replied, keeping my eyes straight ahead. Seeing that I knew there'd be a follow-up question, I quickly added, "The Spin was called to the scene, though, and this one should be relatively easy for them to manage. Goblins wearing mobster suits and carrying tommy guns in New York-New York is almost dying to be a show, after all."

Silver grunted.

If nothing else, the ubers *had* brought some very interesting elements that could be exploited on the Strip. The wizard battles at Excalibur, pixie dust beast showdowns, and the zombie hunt out in the desert were just three ideas. Actually, Paula *did* make the zombie hunting one a reality. But now we had a new wrinkle in the form of gangster goblins. It was silly, but the normals would eat it up.

"You're fucking hiding something, you dickless wonder," EQK chirped out of the blue. "I don't know what it is, but something's off about you."

"Whatever do you mean, EQK?" I replied with an innocent look. "I have told you all I know."

"Don't try to play me, ass nugget," he shot back. "I practically invented bullshit."

"Technically, EQK," Silver countered, "it's well documented that bulls invented it."

"Fuck you, fang face. He knows what I mean."

Obviously, EQK was picking up on my demeanor. Everyone else in the room was too self-involved to notice that I was acting any differently. Or, more likely, they didn't care. But EQK was a pixie, and pixies were known for seeking out weak spots in a person. They watched you, studied you, and kept tabs on any changes in your behavior so they could pounce at the tiniest sign of weakness. This was something I should have taken into account when I decided to go stone-faced in this meeting.

"I'm fine," I replied without changing my voice or posture. "I just woke up with a headache and it's not improved any."

"Sorry to hear that," said O, sounding genuine. "You should request one of your mages to remedy it."

"I hadn't considered that, sir," I acknowledged. "I'll do so after this meeting."

"You guys can cure headaches?" Zack asked. "I get migraines all the time."

"Cure? No. But we can help alleviate symptoms from time to time."

"So can ibuprofen," Silver said with a sigh.

"Doesn't work for migraines," Zack argued.

"Fine, then take an aspirin or get a prescription," Silver groaned. "The point is that you *don't* need to resort to magic over every little thing."

"Magic is just as worthwhile as—"

"He's lying," EQK said loudly enough to be heard but quietly enough to make everyone listen. You see, when

EQK usually spoke, it was at a volume that makes you want to ignore him. Well, that and the content was usually vulgar and unhelpful. But when he spoke at a reasonable decibel, people paid attention. "I know he's lying."

"Who?" said Zack.

"Eaten Dix, of course," grumbled EQK. "For fuck's sake, Zackhole, where have you been?"

"Watch it, pixie," Zack growled back. "I don't like being called names."

EQK snorted. "So?"

Fine. The pixie was on to me, but I was going to continue playing it aloof. He couldn't prove anything as long as I kept my mouth shut. EQK had nothing to stand on, unless I tripped up.

"Is there something more you wish to tell us, Mr. Dex?" O asked.

"No, sir," I replied with a shrug. "I have no idea what Director EQK is talking about."

"There!" EQK said. "Did you not hear that, you mentally deranged pecker sniffers?"

The other Directors collectively sighed.

"Hear what?" Silver asked after a moment.

"That one-balled foreskin feeler *didn't* call me any names."

I felt all eyes turn back to me. I couldn't *see* them, but I sensed it as plain as if there were no mist separating us.

"I'm merely trying to be more respectful, sir," I defended myself. "Things have gotten a little out of hand over the last few weeks and I can't help but feel like I'm partially to blame."

"Admirable," announced Zack.

"Thank you, sir."

"You're full of shit, sphincter lips," EQK jeered. "A person doesn't just go from winning a *Joke-Off* against an uber pixie to suddenly being nice. Doesn't happen."

"It doesn't for pixies, maybe," I debated. "But I'm not a pixie." I then held up my hand before he could retaliate. "However, if it will make you feel better, I do find you to be a taint-meandering, odoriferously leathered clit."

"Mr. Dex!" shouted O.

"Shut up, mage quiff," EQK barked at O. "Dex just called me a pixie-worthy name right there. Proves to me that he's not completely lost his marbles." He then leaned forward enough to break the mist, before it covered his face and drowned my memory of what he looked like. "But I'm watching you, Dexless."

That name didn't even make any sense, which told me I had him unbalanced.

Good.

"*Stay behind, Mr. Dex,*" O commanded via a direct connection. "*I wish to speak with you privately.*"

"*Yes, sir,*" I replied, feeling kind of shocked since I'd never been direct-connected before by any of the Directors.

"If there is nothing else for Mr. Dex," O announced, "I suggest we call it a day so that he may get his headache attended to."

One by one, everyone left the meeting until only O and I remained. Was a reprimand in my immediate future? For O's sake, I hoped not because I was already on the brink of telling him and the rest of the world to fuck off.

"How are you doing, Mr. Dex?" he asked, sounding sincere.

I shifted uncomfortably, not expecting this type of question.

"I'm okay," I answered, feeling somewhat dubious. "Uh…how are you?"

O chuckled. "I'm not asking to establish pleasantries here. I'm asking out of genuine concern for the well-being of an officer who works for me."

Okay, now I was really confused.

Did he sense something was off with me, too? He *was* a mage, after all. Maybe they could pick up on things from a distance? No, Rachel would have warned me about that.

"Ah," I said, trying to play it aloof. "A little anxiety, I suppose. Playing with ubers over these last number of months has taken its toll." I shrugged. "Seems like it has on everyone."

"Indeed." He let out a long breath. "I trust that you have been keeping the outburst from EQK a few meetings back confidential?"

"You would need to narrow that down, sir."

Another chuckle. "Fair enough, fair enough. I'm speaking about the meeting when you told us about Rot."

"Ah, yes." I hadn't really been overly quiet about it, but why tell him that? "I only share information with my crew that will help them to effectively do their jobs, sir."

"That's a cryptic response, Mr. Dex."

"Yes, sir."

I got the feeling he was nodding.

"Sir," I asked suddenly, "did you ever walk the beat?"

JOHN P. LOGSDON & CHRISTOPHER P. YOUNG

"Of course," he answered, sounding distant. "A long time ago."

"Where were you stationed?"

"A few places, actually. New York, Tucson, Bangkok, and London. I even did a couple of years in the Netherworld PPD."

"Cool," I said. "I kind of liked London."

"Same here," he answered. "That's where I met Tristan Montague, in fact." He paused. "I believe you know him?"

"We've run into each other before."

"Well, we trained together in the early days, before the war. Never served together, but I could tell some stories. I don't believe I've ever met a mage who loved blowing things up as much as Tristan." He laughed the laugh of a man reminiscing. "Anyway, why do you ask?"

"Just curious." I adjusted in my chair. "Were you ever chief?"

"Twice," he replied, sounding like it was his turn to feel my line of questions were dubious. "Where are you going with this, Mr. Dex?"

"I don't want this to come off as me being antagonistic, sir, because I truly don't mean it that way," I assured him, "but how did you handle it when your Directors withheld information that you felt put you and your officers in harm's way?"

I heard his knuckles rapping gently on the table in front of him. Obviously, I'd struck a nerve. If he took my question as intended, maybe I'd get a decent answer; if not, he'd likely chew me out.

"Take this for what it is, Mr. Dex," he said finally, using a slow cadence. "Decisions are made that seem right at the time, but unexpected variables arise and dash all hope." He continued tapping the table. "When you learn of fresh challenges, your perspective changes and you find yourself doing the unthinkable. It's done for the greater good...or at least you believe that to be true, but you still have to live with those decisions."

I had no idea what the hell he was talking about, unless this was just daily cop stuff. Half my life was doing the unthinkable while believing it was for the greater good, or at least hoping it was. But I had a feeling O was talking about something deeper than that.

"Is this about the ubers?" I ventured.

"It's about the depth of authority that one at my level deals with, Mr. Dex. When you were a civilian, you had responsibilities just like everyone else. But then you became an officer and those responsibilities grew. Now that you're a chief, they're even greater than before." He sniffed. "Imagine the level of responsibility you'll feel on the day you sit in my chair."

That cut to the core, and he was right. The shit I dealt with as chief towered over what I'd had to deal with before I was ever a cop. The line between life and death was often a decision away for me these days.

"I understand," I said, though I truly did not want to admit it. "Thanks for your candor."

"It's the least I can do," he said. "Do note that all of us *want* to provide you with everything you need to get your job done safely and effectively. We don't go out of our way to see our officers destroyed, after all. But there are times when too much knowledge can actually be more detrimental than not enough."

I couldn't fathom that being the case, but I decided to let it go for now. It wasn't like my arguing the point would do anything but turn a reasonable conversation into a pissing contest.

"We'll do the best we can, then," I announced, feeling a little invigorated.

"I know, Mr. Dex," he replied, "and you should know that we *do* appreciate it."

## CHAPTER 14

*I* honestly had no desire to meet with my crew at the moment. Tensions were high and I was the primary cause of that. Plus, I knew Chuck and Serena would sense the vampire side of me, especially because I was certainly going to have a territorial reaction to them. How they managed to be around each other was beyond me. I guess it's just something they dealt with growing up. As for the mages, Jasmine already knew something was up, as did Rachel, obviously, but I had the feeling Griff would pick up on the truth of things immediately. He'd been around for a long time, after all, and he was obviously the leader in the Vegas PPD when it came to mages. Rachel and Jasmine were his peers as officers, yes, but they deferred to him nine times out of ten when it came to magic. Translation: Griff knew his shit, and that meant he'd spot me a mile away.

Regardless, the meeting had to happen.

The only thing I could hope for was that they'd maintain their professionalism.

That went double for me.

I walked into the conference room and took my spot at the head of the table. It felt like I'd walked into a vat of gel. The emotions were ripping at me from all angles, each jockeying for position at the top of the ladder.

I had to keep it together.

"Before we get started," I announced, keeping my eyes on the table, "I just want to say that I know I've been a bit irritable this morning." I glanced at Rachel. "We had an argument." Obviously a lie. "The fact, though, is that our relationship should have no bearing on our professional life. We will resolve that and learn to separate church and state, as it were." I cleared my throat and sat up in a more positive way. "That said, please accept my apologies on the matter and let's get back to work."

Nobody said anything, but as I scanned the room it was obvious everyone knew something was up. I would have to take control of this quickly.

"Okay, what's the word on the goblins?" I asked, looking at Chuck. "Find anything?"

"Uh..." He shook himself back from wherever his mind had drifted. "Sorry. Nothing much, really. Spanx essentially detailed the same thing he'd already told you."

"We called down to the Netherworld PPD to see if they could give us information on past crimes," added Serena, sounding like she was fighting to keep control of her voice. I felt the same pull toward her that I'd felt toward Felicia earlier, but this was more refined. Still sexual, but not as animalistic. "There weren't any

82

correlations with topside people at all. In fact, based on his record and the data in the central archives, this was the first time Spanx had ever been topside."

"Interesting."

It begged the question why our mystery man would summon a goblin who was unfamiliar with how things worked up here. The only thing I could think of was it had to do with his ability to use magic. But Mr. Mystery had to know that we would be able to defuse that in relatively quick order. It wasn't like we were all rookies, after all.

"Theories?" I asked the room.

Griff leaned back and crossed his arms, letting out a slow breath. It was good to see him back to one hundred percent. The werewolf attack he'd endured a few weeks back had been pretty brutal, and it had taken him quite a while to recover.

"I propose that we have another ubernatural here," he remarked. "It reminds me of the mage Reese, in fact. Not that ·I believe this person is a mage. There isn't enough information to make that claim as yet. But I sense that we are being tested."

"My thoughts exactly," I concurred. "I just hope there aren't any demon batteries this time around."

"Or worse," noted Felicia.

I looked at her with a forced grin. "There's worse?"

"Ian, sweetie," Lydia interrupted over the room's speaker, "it appears that we have a werebear gorging at the Bacchanal Buffet at Caesar's Palace."

"You're kidding," I grumbled.

"Sorry, puddin'."

My head fell forward and I groaned, wanting to just grab the table and start swinging it around.

I was going to have to take up meditation or something.

Slowly, I glanced up at Griff and said, "Looks like we're in for another of Mr. Mystery's tests."

CHAPTER 15

"So, how did it go with the Directors?" Rachel asked on our ride over to Caesar's.

"Exactly as you'd expect," I answered, right before turning onto East Flamingo. "We were all just sharing surface stuff. EQK *did* suspect me, but nobody else did."

I then thought back to my conversation with O, wondering if I should share that with Rachel or not. O didn't expressly say I shouldn't, but it was kind of a personal chat. I glanced over at her and decided she was the only real person I could confide in. The more she knew, the more she could help me through whatever the hell I was dealing with here.

"O direct-connected and asked me to stay after the others left," I said slowly. "He just wanted to check on my well-being."

She shifted. "Do you think he knows?"

"No," I answered, but then added, "Mages can't tell that stuff from a distance, can they?"

"Depends on the distance," she said. "Definitely not through a connection like you guys use in there, though."

I nodded. It didn't seem likely, but I had to make sure. While mages could read energy signatures just fine, they were only as good with body language as anyone else. Pixies won the award for picking up on physical cues, but everyone else was average at that game.

"Thought so. Anyway, he was pointing out how difficult it is to be in his position." We stopped at the light across from Caesar's. "Compared it to my position as chief. Responsibility differences from being an officer and all that."

"Right."

"It wasn't much more than that," I said, shrugging as the light turned green, "but it was enough to make me feel like he genuinely gave a shit, ya know?"

"Either that or he was suspicious and trying to see what kind of information you were hiding." She scraped the leather on her pants with her fingernail. "One of the techniques mages use to gain information is to confide in a person, Ian. It gets you to think they're on your side, then you let down your guard so they can unravel deeper thoughts you may have."

I laughed. "Doesn't everyone do that?"

"Well, yes," she admitted, "but remember that mages use distraction to fool the eye just as much as they use real magic." She started scratching at the leather again. "Did you tell him anything that you wouldn't have told him if all the Directors had been present?"

"Nothing that I can think of," I replied, thinking

through our conversation. "If anything, *he* was the one spilling his guts."

"So you didn't ask any questions or anything?" she pressed, but she did so gently. "It's probably nothing, but I'm just checking."

"I asked him if he ever walked the beat and if he was ever chief." We found a place to park and I shut down the Aston Martin. Usually, I'd just go with valet parking, but I knew my crew was already on the scene. They could handle the werebear. "He just rattled off the places he'd served, told me that he'd trained with Tristan Montague, and then went into a long diatribe about responsibilities."

"Why would he bring Monty into the discussion?"

I looked at her. "I don't know."

"I do," she declared. "Because O, Monty, and Griff all trained together back then."

"So?"

"So O's telling you that he knows Griff very well."

"Ah," I said, sitting back in my seat. Then, I looked at her again. "He was?"

Rachel gave me a dull look and sighed. I tilted my head and showed her my tired eyes. While she may have just had some epiphany about all of this, I didn't know what the hell she was talking about.

Obviously, she recognized she was teetering on being too impatient. She put her hand on mine and smiled.

"I don't know for sure," she said, "but my guess is that O *did* notice something is up with you. Probably not the magic, but rather some other tell…" She paused. "You didn't have your fangs out, did you?"

I grimaced at her.

"Right, no. Sorry." She sniffed. "Well, again, he probably noticed something, and my guess is that he assumed you'd tell us about his conversation."

"Why would he assume that?"

"Because you have constantly been saying how you keep your officers informed," she replied. "Mages don't miss things like that, Ian. We listen."

"Good to know," I said in a measured tone.

"I *am* a mage, remember?" She smirked. "Again, I don't know for certain what O's plan is, but if he brought up Monty out of the blue, that means he's tying something together. My guess is he's telling you that Griff might be able to help you out."

I shook my head at this level of deduction. It made no sense to me, but I was pretty new to this advanced level of magic. Regardless of the fact that the magical element itself wasn't where Rachel and O learned this aspect of maging, it was still a mage tactic. One that clearly came from years of study.

"I don't pretend to know how you unraveled that yarn," I declared as I reached for the door handle, "and I honestly have a hard time believing it to be accurate, but I'll take your word for it." I stopped just before getting out of the car. "Wait. If you're right, and O *does* want me to talk to Griff about whatever it is that's going on with me, could that mean that Griff reports things back to O?"

Rachel went to open her mouth but stopped and looked away with concern.

"Shit," she said. "You might be right."

## CHAPTER 16

*B*y the time we got to the buffet in Caesar's, there was a pretty large crowd standing around watching the show.

Paula was already there, arms crossed, but I put out my hand at her to signal that she should hold her complaints until the werebear was contained. Frankly, I couldn't see a way for her to spin this one. Goblins in gangster suits at New York-New York was a match made in heaven, but a werebear tearing through the Bacchanal Buffet at Caesar's Palace? Not so much.

Oh well.

Not my problem.

What *was* my problem was in the process of rushing toward the dessert section. A fully morphed werebear who I'd guess stood about eight feet tall on his...no, on *her* hind legs. Great, a lady bear. Hopefully there weren't any baby bears around or this would really suck.

*"Rachel and I have arrived,"* I announced through the

89

connector. *"I see a female bear here. Someone please tell me there aren't any cubs."*

*"No cubs, Chief,"* answered Chuck, *"but this bear is acting like there are. Nobody can even get close to the food. She's going berserk."*

*"Fortunately, she's keeping inside the buffet area,"* noted Jasmine.

That was good, at least. A wandering bear wreaking havoc was far worse than a stationary bear who was defending her territory. Defense we could manage. Chasing a bear through a hotel full of normals, on the other hand, was not a pleasant prospect.

*"We have to keep her contained here,"* I said more for myself than anyone else. *"I want coverage on the main entrances. Warren, are you here?"*

*"Yeah, Chief?"*

*"Good. Work with hotel security and get everyone back. This isn't going to be pretty, unless the bear decides to give up."* As if on cue, the creature roared and smashed down on a table. *"Doesn't look like that's going to happen."*

*"Got it, Chief,"* he replied.

I knew Warren wasn't one who was fond of standing toe to toe with anything overly threatening. He was great with skeletons because they had no muscles and were really easy to destroy, but a werebear was covered in muscle and was vicious as fuck. One slap from her massive claws and Warren would be deader than dead. He'd be halved.

*"Everyone else, cover me and Rachel."*

"What?" she choked aloud. "I don't want to go in there with that thing."

I squinted at her. "You're a cop, Rachel. It's your job."

"You know, I get that you want to make sure you're not seen as playing favorites with me," she remarked, "but that doesn't mean you throw me under the bus at every turn either."

"Wait a second here," I said as a grin formed on my face. "Are you afraid of werebears?"

"Only when they're attacking," she replied. "Big claws, big jaws, big muscles, able to rip us to shreds without even breaking a sweat, have a tendency to—"

"They can sweat?"

"Uh...I don't know, asshole." She scowled. "That's not the point."

I could have done without the "asshole" remark, but I had it coming, and it was an indicator that Rachel wasn't currently fawning over me.

"We're doing this, Rachel," I said firmly.

"Ugh."

We walked toward the werebear with measured steps. It followed us with red eyes. They weren't smoldering, but I had a feeling that when they did, they'd overshadow my newfound ability in that area.

A low growl escaped her maw and her paws flexed.

She was readying to attack.

*"She's going to hit us here in a second, gang,"* I connected. *"Get your guns and spells ready. Do. Not. Miss. We can't afford a stray spell or bullet striking a normal. Is that clear?"*

They affirmed my command in unison.

I directed Rachel to go to the right while I went left. The werebear kept her eyes on me. At least that would buy Rachel some time to get her magic flowing.

The rumble of the beast's throat was getting louder and she began scratching the table top she was standing behind. I honestly had little desire to feel what that table was experiencing, but I had the sneaking suspicion a swipe or two was in my future.

"Okay, girl," I said in a soothing voice as I held my hands up in a show of submission, "everything is going to be okay. We just want to talk."

"No you don't," she objected, her voice grating so badly that it was barely understandable. "You want to take away my food. I'm not stupid."

"It's not *your* food, I'm afraid," I replied as diplomatically as I could. "This place belongs to the hotel. All those people out there have paid to eat here."

Her eyes swept over the crowd menacingly. "Then they will die."

"You can't kill all of them," I was quick to point out. "Yeah, you're big and strong, but even you can't take down that many people."

Her growl became more pronounced.

"Maybe not," she said, her nostrils flaring, "but I can sure as fuck take you down."

With a speed that no creature of that size should possess, she launched her full weight at me with claws extended.

"Shit!" I yelled as we crashed to the ground.

# CHAPTER 17

*N*ow, I'm not going to sit here and tell you that when the anger rose up in me, I felt my muscles bulging to the point where my clothes ripped. And I'm not going to say that I saw nothing but red due to the billowing of rage filling my world. And I'm *definitely* not going to say that my skin had turned green.

But I was pretty pissed off and that caused something I didn't expect.

I became a vampwolfmagixie.

You read that right.

So much for my assumption that when one of the facets of my amalgamiteness came out to play, the others receded.

My teeth burst forth, my strength easily doubled, magic filled me like I'd hit a beer bong full of elixir… magic bong?, and I felt a rush of foul language racing to get in line at my vocal cords.

To make matters worse, the damn werebear was up and swiping at me while my mages peppered it with fire, ice, and electricity. Chuck and Felicia were plugging it with .50 caliber rounds, too. This was worse because I got to feel all of the fallout from that.

Even more fun was the fact that the damn bear wasn't being impacted by any of it. The bullets were bouncing off…and the damn thing *had no shield*.

"Hold your fucking fire, you jizz guzzling fucktardth!" I hollered, surprised that I could say the letter 'z' without lisping it.

They stopped and I felt instantly bad for calling them that.

The bear looked completely baffled by my outburst. She even gazed down at me and tilted her head. Then, she squinted.

"Are those fangs?" she asked, leaning in.

"Yeth," I replied and then grabbed her by the side and launched her off me.

I'm not shitting you when I say "launched" either. Believe me, I was more shocked about this than anyone. That bear felt like she weighed next to nothing. Obviously, my werewolf strength was intense, especially when mixed with my vampire power.

She crashed into one of the buffet walls, grunting on impact.

Then she looked over at me with fear in her eyes.

"That'th right, bisch," I lisped, wishing I knew more words with the letter 'z' in them. I got to my feet. "You athked for the pain, and now I'm going to bring it."

"What the hell are you?" she asked as her eyes darted

around, clearly seeking for a means of escape. "I thought you were just a vampire, but—"

"I'm *not* a vampire," I grunted, my shoulders slumping.

She pointed at me. "But you have fangs."

"Okay, okay," I groaned. "Tho I'm partthially a vampire, you pedantic phalluth."

"What did you call me?" she asked, perplexed.

"Forget it."

"Wait," she said after a moment. "Vampires aren't as strong as you."

"That'th becauthe—" I paused and pulled my teeth back in. "That's because I'm really an amalgamite."

"What's that?"

"It's a…" I stopped and took a deep breath. "It's not important right now. The fact is that you are under arrest." I squared my shoulders. "Now, you can either come quietly—"

"Oh, no," she said, waving a paw at me, "I'm a screamer."

"What?" I then sighed as I caught what had just transpired. Wasn't it *me* who was supposed to be the horndog? Wasn't *I* the one who always had a juvenile thought when something sounded just wrong enough? "I didn't mean it that way, you undescended testicle."

She put her paws on her hips. This looked really odd, since she was still fully in bear mode.

"What's with the name calling?"

"Are you going to come—" I held up a hand at her warningly as I rethought my wording. "Are you going to surrender or am I going to have to kill you?"

She glanced around again until her eyes locked on

Rachel. Then she began to grin. Now, it should be noted that when a werebear grins it's not something you would consider cute. In fact, it looks rather menacing.

This wasn't going to go well.

CHAPTER 18

*R*achel spotted the problem the instant I did, but she wasn't as fast as the bear. Thus, she got swept up, spun around, and used as a human shield.

My eyes did that smoldering thing again.

"What are you going to do?" the bear said as her claws rested on Rachel's neck. "All it will take is one quick swipe to make her blood spill. Is that what you want?"

"The better question," I replied, fighting to stay calm, "is what do *you* want?"

She cocked her head toward one of the buffet stations. "My food to be left alone."

I frowned at her. That couldn't possibly be all there was to this. It made no sense. Okay, so maybe a bear would love to have an unlimited food supply. I wouldn't know, to be honest. I'm not a bearologist, or whatever the hell they're called. But this wasn't simply a bear. This was a werebear, meaning that when this was all said and done, she was going to go back to being a human-looking

97

woman. She'd be able to buy normal food or even go to this very buffet and partake without incident.

"Look, Smokey," I insisted, "there's got to be more to this than merely food."

"Did you just call me Smokey?"

"Well, I don't know your actual name, so—"

"So you took it upon yourself to call me Smokey, as in Smokey the Bear, right?" Then she shook her head in disbelief. "That's just rude."

"It is," Rachel said, giving me a disappointed look. "You should apologize, Ian."

"What?"

"Seriously. You don't just go and call someone by a name like that." Even though her life was in the balance and a wearbear had its claws on her throat, Rachel had managed to cross her arms. "Apologize, please."

I squinted. "You had no problem with me calling her a testicle."

"Because that wasn't directly a slight on her species. Calling her Smokey is."

The bear looked at me, then at Rachel, and then did that wicked smiling thing again.

"Are you two dating?"

"Apologize, Ian," Rachel reiterated.

"Fine," I exploded and then glared at the bear. "I'm sorry I called you Smokey, okay?"

Smokey began to laugh.

Yes, I know I was still thinking of her as Smokey, but I had nothing else to go on. Besides, I'm allowed to be as rude as I wish in the privacy of my own thoughts.

"You *are* dating." Smokey continued giggling. "That

means you'll not do a damn thing to me as long as I have her in my clutches."

"He sure won't," Rachel agreed. Then she winked at me and added, "But, I will."

With that, Rachel spun in and toward the bear's armpit and slipped from her grasp, diving away as quickly as she could.

Smokey roared and started to reach out, but my magic was faster than her attack.

In less than a second, I had pulled up my hand and unleashed wave after wave of fire mixed with energy. The energy pulse lifted the bear into the air and the fire cooked her midsection as she screamed and fought to get away. When she finally passed out, I flicked my wrist and sent her flying toward the wall.

She struck it with a resounding thud.

A smear of blood trailed her as she slid down, coming to her final rest on the ground.

Smokey was dead.

I immediately shut down my magic and unleashed a flurry of whispered curses that would have made EQK blush.

Bottom line: I was busted.

Then I slowly looked at each person on my team, in turn. Not a single jaw was closed, except for Griff's. Instead of shock and awe, he looked concerned.

Great.

## CHAPTER 19

Security dispersed the crowd and shut down the buffet for a bit. They were going to have to give the area a thorough cleaning anyway, so it had to be done.

Serena was working with Warren to do some study on the werebear. Well, previous werebear. The woman had turned back to looking like a standard human now.

The rest of the PPD crew stuck null zones up around the perimeter as well, just to further deter prying eyes. We couldn't do a hidden zone because people would wonder where the heck the buffet disappeared to. That would only serve to make Paula Rose's already difficult job even more trying.

"How the hell do you expect me to spin this one, Ian?" she complained. "A freaking werebear tearing up a buffet and you with your magical light show…I mean, come on!"

My first reaction was to pick her up, growl at her, and bite her neck. Rachel's arm on my shoulder served to remind me that wouldn't be such a grand idea.

Still, I wasn't going to be browbeaten by Paula today.

"I understand you have a difficult job," I said in a steady voice, "but it's a job *you* chose to do. If you can't figure out a way to spin things, you may want consider finding something less challenging."

Her mouth went slack as her eyes bulged.

"What did you just say to me?"

I pushed past her, ignoring her question, and walked out to where the rest of my team had gathered. Rachel was giggling during the walk and Paula was yelling after me, using rather derogatory language. I ignored them both.

"Chief…" started Chuck, but I held up my hand to silence him.

"Everyone, follow me," I commanded.

The walk to the exit was done in complete silence. I had reported to Lydia that the situation was resolved.

"*Rachel,*" I said finally through a direct-connection, "*please have everyone shut down their connectors completely.*"

"*Why?*"

I glanced at her.

"*Okay,*" she said, putting her hands up in surrender. "*Jeez.*"

"*Make sure that only* they *hear you. I don't want Lydia to know.*"

"*I don't…*" She paused. "*Oh, wait. I get it. Hadn't thought of that.*"

I disconnected from her and continued walking until we had gotten out to the parking garage. Then I headed down to the lowest level and off to the far corner.

Once there, I requested that the mages put up a null zone and a hidden zone around us.

They complied, but I still didn't feel safe talking about what was going on.

The fact was that our connectors were supposed to be active devices only, meaning that Lydia or anyone else couldn't hear anything we said unless we actively invited them into our skulls. But I had no proof of this level of security. For all I knew, everything that Rachel and I had been saying to each other since getting injected with vampire venom could be in Lydia's banks already.

Just in case, I thought the best way to ensure there could be no listening in would be to jump to a place where I was certain there was no connectivity.

"Everyone link hands," I stated, grabbing Rachel's hand on my left and Griff's on my right. Once everyone was linked, I said, "I'm going to explain everything, but not here."

"Then where?" asked Felicia.

"Just be ready for anything," I answered and then closed my eyes, took a deep breath, and said, "I want me some valkyrie lovin'."

CHAPTER 20

y crew was gazing around the large arena
that made up the seventh level of "Hell." It
wasn't really Hell, of course, but Dante considered it such
in his *Divine Comedy*.

This was the level that belonged to the valkyries.

Yes, I'm talking about the babes who got all dressed up
in armor and walked around the battlefields deciding who
lived and who died. And when I say "babes," I thoroughly
mean that. We're talking seven-foot-tall musclebound
ladies in full battle gear.

"*Drool*," said The Admiral as the lead valkyrie, Valerie,
began sauntering over.

"*Shut up*," I admonished my dick.

"He's right, though," Rachel noted in a whisper. "Holy
shit pickles, Ian. If I knew they looked like this, I would
have joined you."

"*Really?*" The Admiral squeaked.

"Really?" I squeaked an instant later.

"Totally," Rachel answered us both. "We'll have to discuss this at some point."

*"Well, my feeling is that—"*

*"Not now, idiot!"*

*"Oh, right. Sorry. I'll just hide out here in the dark and wait."*

I rolled my eyes and sighed. Why couldn't I be normal? Not like normal-normal. I still wanted to remain a supernatural, but couldn't I at least not have a talking dick?

"Ian Dex," Valerie said as her eyes landed on me after she studied my crew, "have you returned for another try?"

"He sure has," answered Rachel with a big grin.

"No," I stated an instant later, pushing Rachel back. "I'm sorry to have intruded on you, Valerie, but I am in need of assistance and this is the only place I could think of where my internal communications device could not be overheard."

She nodded for a moment, though she appeared distracted. I followed her eyes and saw she was looking at Rachel, who was twirling her hair like a schoolgirl who had a crush on her teacher.

"Ugh," I said.

On the one hand, it *was* a major turn on that Rachel found the valkyries to be smokin' hot; on the other hand, there was a time for play and a time for work. Now was *not* a time for play.

*"Speaking of hands,"* The Admiral chimed in, *"I don't suppose I could borrow one of yours for a few minutes? Or Rachel's? Or Valerie's?"*

"I vote Valerie's," Rachel coaxed.

*"Both of you shut the hell up right now!"*

"Why did that one use my name?" Valerie asked, pointing at Rachel. Then she glanced at me for a moment and then back at Rachel. "Is she the one who made it so you couldn't perform?"

Chuck, Felicia, Warren, Serena, and Jasmine all giggled. Griff was too classy to stoop low enough to find something such as this humorous. Rachel was too enthralled to even catch on.

I groaned and set about introducing everyone to Valerie as the rest of the valkyries fanned out behind her.

"For the love of…" Rachel breathed out heavily. "You're all gorgeous."

"You can say that again," agreed Serena. "I wouldn't mind playing in this level for a while. Can anyone apply to work here?"

*"I know of a few openings I could fill,"* The Admiral was quick to note.

"I don't think it works that way, Serena," I answered for Valerie.

"Yes, anyone can apply to work here," Valerie said, proving I was wrong. She studied Serena for a moment. "You are a little on the small side, though. I'm afraid we would only be able to offer you pleasuring duties."

I raised an eyebrow at this.

Okay, yes, I was currently in the middle of a mental breakdown, but managing pleasuring duties for valkyries sounded like a dream job.

*"Now, you're talking,"* The Admiral Agreed.

Serena's voice remained steady. "Pleasuring duties?"

"Yes," Valerie replied without inflection. "You would feed us, bathe us, give us massages, and meet our more carnal needs."

"Where do I sign up?" said a voice that I suddenly realized was my own. I shook myself back to reality. "Shit. Sorry."

Valerie gave me a wicked grin. "You are the one that *we* wish to pleasure, remember?"

"*Even better*," The Admiral sang.

Yes, sang.

"Oh yeah," Rachel said like she was all for that plan, "we're totally going to discuss this again."

Things were getting a little crazy at the moment. This made sense, seeing that there was a fair bit of horniness that came with being a PPD officer, but had everyone on my team suddenly forgotten that I had fired off some major magic against a werebear not too long ago?

One look at Griff and Chuck told me that they remembered. Of course, they were gay, so the prospect of pleasuring valkyries wasn't as appealing to them as it was to the rest of us. The ladies on my squad were all bisexual, though. I knew this because they had essentially admitted it during the battle with our first ubernatural a number of months back. Well, Rachel, Jasmine, and Felicia had anyway. Serena's interest in other women was kind of new to me, but seeing as how she'd just requested a job application, it was immediately apparent what her interests were. Warren had once claimed that he was pansexual. At first I thought this meant he liked screwing cooking equipment, but I learned later that he just had no issues with boning men, women, or even supers who were in their supernatural forms. He wasn't into doing weird crap with regular animals or anything, though. He'd been clear about that.

Now, me? My sexuality was pretty straightforward. I was *buy*-sexual. If I couldn't get sex, I'd buy it.

"Valerie," I spoke up, taking her eyes off my crew, "something has happened to me and I really need to tell my agents what's going on. Now, I know they're all incredibly horny—you and your beautiful ladies will do that to people—but I have to talk to these guys right now."

The look of concern on her face was kind of touching, if I was being honest.

*"I think it'd be cool if she were kind of touching me right about now,"* The Admiral stated out of the blue.

*"Would you* please *shut up?"*

"Are you well, Ian Dex?" Valerie asked.

"Not really," I replied honestly.

Then I went on to explain everything that had happened to me, from the djinn fucking with my head, to the vampire biting me, and finally on to how I learned that my amalgamite bits and pieces were seemingly forming into one.

"You've already seen what I can do with magic," I pointed out to my crew, "but there's more."

I showed them my fangs.

"Sexy," meowed Valerie.

"It really is," agreed Serena.

"Totally," whispered Warren.

"Ew," I said.

"Now, I must admit that I find this rather appealing," Griff remarked. Chuck looked at him. "Sorry, Charles, but you know how I have a thing for you vampires."

I threw up a little in my mouth. "Double ew."

CHAPTER 21

We had all taken seats and the questioning began. Unlike the Directors, I didn't want to keep my crew in the dark, but I was also a bit worried about providing too much information.

Valerie kept the valkyries away, giving us time to work through things. Since we weren't being judged in battle, I knew Valerie and her crew were forbidden to read our thoughts, so I didn't have to worry about that. She'd probably overhear our words, though.

Ah well. That couldn't be helped. Besides, who was she going to tell?

"Have you ever been bitten by a vampire before?" asked Griff.

"No."

"What about a wolf?"

"I don't…" I paused and thought about that. "Actually, more than once over the years, yes. We've all taken down

111

a number of them while on the beat. I've fought vampires, too, of course, but never been bitten. Werewolves, though? Definitely."

"But a werewolf bite is not the same as a vampire bite," Chuck was quick to point out. "Werewolves don't inject venom."

Griff gave his partner an appraising look. "It's a fair point, Charles."

"I've also been hit by tons of magic over the years, Griff," I stated. "That never turned me into a mage."

"True."

"And we all know that I've recently had a *Joke-Off* with a pixie. Again, nothing came of that." I shook my head and sighed. "No, it was definitely the venom that sparked everything. Possibly the djinn, too. I'm not sure if that played into things any more than just making me disoriented enough to allow the vampire to have a snack."

Again, though, it brought up the question as to how the djinn was able to mess with my head in the first place. That had never happened before either.

"Do you think the djinn was an uber?" asked Felicia.

"No," I replied as the answer dawned on me. "I think the djinn was given stronger powers, just like the goblin mage and the werebear."

"Ah," said Griff while rubbing his beard. "That makes sense."

Mr. Mystery was doling out powers to key people in order to make my life miserable. But why? I wasn't about to ask that question aloud because people would just claim that I'd boned Mrs. Mystery or something. It didn't matter how many times I'd told them that I didn't do that kind of thing, they still made the assumption.

"Did you bone Mrs. Mystery, Ian?" asked Jasmine.

So much for that.

"No, I did not bone Mrs. Mystery," I answered dryly. "Or, if I did, I didn't know it was Mrs. Mystery. I'm pretty careful about that sort of thing, *as you know*."

"My assumption is that we have another ubernatural who is bent on destroying you in a way that is not so direct," announced Griff, clearly ignoring the side conversation. "But why this person would go out of their way to make you stronger is beyond my ability to understand. It would seem to me that weakening you is far more sensible."

I crossed my legs and flicked a lint ball off my knee.

"Exactly what I'm thinking, Griff."

"Maybe the guy thought it'd make you weaker?" suggested Warren. We all looked at him. "Well, think about it. If you wanted to take a guy out, you'd just kill him, right?"

"But a bite wouldn't kill him," remarked Chuck. "In fact…" He slowly looked up at me. "In fact," he said again, "a vampire injecting venom is for the purpose of controlling the victim. He wasn't trying to kill you, Chief. He wanted you as his slave."

"Ew," I choked.

"Not *that* kind of slave, Chief."

"Oh, right."

A slave? To do what? Comb his hair? Help him pick out nice suits? I *was* good at that, but it seemed like a big risk just to get a personal shopper. But what else would a vampire need a slave for? They already had everything.

I was being stupid.

He wanted me to serve his nefarious intentions. I was strong. I was fast. I healed quickly. Basically, I was a weapon, and if whoever this guy was wanted to cause some major damage, he'd have to…

A thought struck.

"So the vampire who bit me would have to be the guy trying to lord over me, right?" I was staring at Chuck.

"Yeah."

"But he seemed so freaked out when I turned on him."

"That doesn't surprise me, Chief," Chuck said. "Vampires aren't supposed to do the old venom trick anymore, but imagine doing it and finding out that the person you bit can rip you in two? It's like his venom failed to put you under his spell. In fact, all it really accomplished was building him an enemy that was stronger than he could ever hope to be."

"But the goblin and the djinn and the werebear," I said, feeling confused. "They had power boosts, too."

"That's because the infused venom *will* improve your power," Chuck explained. "I'm guessing this guy didn't know all the powers you already had. The weird thing is that it's also supposed to have made you loyal to him. Clearly, that didn't happen."

Rachel leaned forward and put her elbows on her knees.

"Are you saying that Spanx didn't tell us who the vampire is because he was really covering for him?"

"Possibly," Chuck replied with a shrug. "It could also be that he genuinely doesn't know."

This new bit of information put us all into thought. If the vampire was really doing all this through a bite, why wouldn't we have seen marks on Spanx's neck? And the same with the djinn. I saw his neck clear as day before I ripped through it. There were no marks.

"Serena," I asked, "were there any holes on Smokey's neck?"

"Ian," warned Rachel.

"Oh, sorry. I mean the werebear's neck."

Serena and Warren shared a look and then both shook their heads.

"Are there any other places that—"

"You have no marks on your neck either, Chief," Felicia noted, pointing at me.

"Because I heal quickly, remember?"

Felicia face-palmed. "Right. Sorry."

"Any large vein will do," Serena stated.

The only way we could know for sure is if we got in touch with Portman at the morgue. We couldn't do that from down here, though. There was no connectivity. But even if we could verify that it was the vampire who bit me, how would we find him? Vegas wasn't huge, but it was big enough for a vampire to hide in. Granted, he *was* going out of his way to pester me, so eventually we'd find him. My worry was how much damage he'd be able to do before then.

There *was* one lead we had, though.

It may have been a slip of the tongue, but Spanx said he was down here on the goblins level when a wizard contacted him. Goblins were known for keeping records of things when it involved agreements—verbal or otherwise. While it was definitely a long shot, it could just be that someone on level six knew the identity of Mr. Mystery.

I knew it was a risk, but my gut said it was time I spoke to Lucy Für.

## CHAPTER 22

"Wait," said Rachel after I'd told her my plan, "why would you want to speak with Lucy Für? She's a demon, not a goblin."

"Yes," I replied, "but Spanx said that he was going to get paid to make a run on New York-New York. That's a verbal contract." I then looked up and pursed my lips. "Hell, maybe he even got a written one. I don't know." I shrugged. "Regardless, there was a contract, and that means demons are involved."

Rachel seemed taken aback by this. "Huh?"

"He is correct," said Griff. "Contractual agreements are the domain of demons, large or small."

"What's the size of the demon have to do with it?" asked Chuck.

Griff appraised his life partner as if judging the man's intellect. The sigh that followed was one of those good-thing-he's-pretty kind of sighs.

"I was speaking about the size of the contract, Charles."

"Ohhh...right."

"At any rate," Griff continued, "the majority of people aren't aware of it, but demons oversee every agreement." He looked studiously from face to face. "*Every* agreement."

I'd known about this because of the notes left to me by Chief Michaels, the man I replaced as the head of the Las Vegas PPD. He'd been my boss for a couple of years, but it wasn't until he'd handed over his notes that I learned a lot more about the happenings in the world...and the Netherworld.

You would have thought the entire demon thing would be common knowledge to the supernatural community, but that would be like expecting everyone to know the ins and outs of the legal system in Dubai. If you were a lawyer in Dubai, you'd know, but if you were just some schmuck living on a farm in Iowa, you'd have no idea. Granted, this was a little different because demons lording over contracts applied to everyone, whereas the legal system in Dubai only applied to people living or vacationing there. The advanced level of secrecy over this wrinkle in the contract code was because people would generally freak out if they knew that demons kept tabs on all contracts. Folks were terrified enough of attorneys. Personally, I would imagine it'd be a good thing if people knew the truth of it. A lot more contracts would be fulfilled, for one, and a lot fewer of them would be ratified in the first place.

I couldn't be too proud of myself, though. The last

time I was here I thought Lucy Für's actual name was Satan.

The chief didn't put any details in his notes about that.

"Shall I request that Lucy Für join us," asked Valerie, "or shall I summon her?"

"Let's request her first," I replied. I didn't know what the difference was between a request and a summons, but Valerie sounded somewhat ominous regarding the summoning option. "Thank you."

She nodded at me and closed her eyes.

Felicia looked like she was about to say something, but I held my finger to my lips. There was no point in distracting a valkyrie as she was attempting to request the presence of a demon, after all.

The room grew dark after a moment.

I felt the hairs on my neck stand up and a shiver ran through my spine. While I still wasn't incredibly versed with magic, I knew what was going on. They were working together to build a portal for Lucy Für to travel through.

Even though the demon queen was only down one level, she could not simply take the stairs.

It would destroy her.

The only way she could escape the nine levels was via a mutual portal or a summoning.

Ah…so that's why Valerie had asked the question before. Whenever one summons an entity from the nine levels, there must be a contract in place or a taking. A taking involves a sacrifice of some sort, making it impossible for the one being summoned to resist. Spanx and his goblin gang, for example, were probably just traveling on contract. The sacrifice option typically happened when those being summoned didn't want to go. This is why the original uber mage, Reese, had been very unpopular with the demons he used as batteries. They didn't want to partake in his power play, but they'd had no choice. Essentially, Reese had kidnapped and enslaved them for his own nefarious gain.

Valkyries were a bit different, too, of course. They traveled wherever there was battle. It was part of their gig. But even they could be summoned to fight, should the proper spells be cast.

But Valerie and Lucy were working together on this portal, which told me the demon queen was willing to help.

We all took a step back as a whirlwind of light began spinning faster and faster. There were multiple colors and the sound of air rushing, to the point of sounding like a small tornado.

Then a blinding light flashed and knocked us all to the ground.

I leaned on one elbow and held my opposite hand up to shield my eyes until the light faded away.

Standing there was Lucy Für.

She was massive. I'm talking five werebears big. She also wasn't what you might call "a looker." Honestly, the first time I saw her those months ago, I'd have sworn she was a dude.

"Ah, Officer Ian Dex," she said after nodding at Valerie. "What a pleasant surprise."

I got to my feet and bowed slightly. "It's…good to see you again, madam."

"I'm sure it is." She raised an eyebrow at me. "Well?"

"Ah, right." I coughed. "There was a contract taken recently by a goblin named Spanx. He was told to go topside, to a hotel in Las Vegas named—"

"New York-New York," she interrupted. "What of it?"

"We need to know who the requesting party is on that contract."

Lucy Für regarded me for a moment. Then she glanced around at the other officers. Finally, she peered at Valerie and grunted.

"You realize that contracts are private matters, yes?"

I nodded.

"Then you must understand that I cannot simply divulge information about the parties involved."

"He's causing all sorts of problems topside," Felicia blurted. "There are already multiple deaths due to what he's done."

Lucy Für tilted her head at Felicia. "So?"

"So," I answered before Felicia could, "it's only a matter of time before he starts summoning demons."

I didn't know that for sure, obviously, but it seemed like a logical step for him. Besides, while demons were quite powerful, it didn't mean they were incapable of feeling concern as well.

"You know this to be true?" she asked me with a directness that made me feel like I had just taken the stand.

"No," I admitted, "but after what I've experienced, I can tell you without a shadow of a doubt that he's capable of it."

She nodded slowly and she released a long breath.

I only caught wind of a hint of it, but that was enough to make me feel like I'd just face-planted in a pile of horse shit. Everyone on my team winced. Warren gagged.

"What is it?" Lucy Für asked.

"Hmmm?" I said, glaring at everyone. "Nothing. Just the memory of a werebear that Mr. Mystery overtook. It was pretty rough. I'd hate to see him do that to a demon."

"Ah, right." Her eyes snapped to mine. "Mr. Mystery?"

"That's what I've been calling him because…" I stopped and looked up at her. "Hold on. You're not going to tell me that's really the guy's name I'm looking for, right?"

It wouldn't be the first time I'd used a name like that about someone I didn't know and it had turned out to be correct. Shitfaced Fred came to mind.

"Oh, I see," she replied with a chuckle. "No, that's *not* his name. I thought you may have been discussing someone else."

I'd have thought that the context would have been sufficient, but who knew how demons thought?

I took a step toward her. "So can you help us or are you going to chance a summoning?"

"You are a clever one, Ian Dex," Lucy Für said as her lip curled into a grin. I'd say it was an evil grin, but being that she was a demon, that seemed redundant. "The vampire you are seeking is named Sylvester Melbourne."

"You're a lifesaver, Lucy," I said with a big smile.

She laughed. "I've been called many things, Ian Dex, but 'lifesaver' is not one of them."

# CHAPTER 23

*I* took Griff aside, away from the rest of the crew. I didn't want to have this discussion, but I needed to know where he stood on things.

"Griff," I said in a measured tone, "how well do you know Director O?"

"We trained together a long time ago."

"Do you—"

"Ian," he said, putting his hand on my shoulder, "if you're asking whether or not he has me in his confidence, the answer is no. I respect the man, but I don't work directly for him. You are the chief of the Las Vegas Paranormal Police Department. Therefore, my loyalties go first to you." He glanced away for a moment. "No, there's more to it than that. The fact is that you're a good man. Rough around the edges, yes, but you always strive to do what is right. I'm not saying that O is any different, but let us just say that my sights are more in line with yours than they are with his."

"Thanks," I said, feeling better about things. "I don't really trust the Directors at the moment."

"Nor should you," he agreed. "Again, I'm certain they have no intentionally negative plans, but the world at their level of power looks incredibly different than it does at our level."

It was spoken like a man who'd attained much more power than he currently had.

My guess was that he'd been highly ranked back in the war, but those were wounds I wasn't willing to open.

"You're a good man, Griff," I said finally.

"The whole team is, Ian."

"Yes."

We walked back into the mix and said our goodbyes to the valkyries and Lucy.

Valerie asked if I would be coming back anytime soon. Rachel answered for me. Let's just say that The Admiral approved of her response.

It also turned out that Lucy and Valerie were friends who hadn't had the chance to spend a lot of time together over the last hundred or so years. I couldn't fathom what they could have had in common, aside from the fact that they were both the leaders of their people. I suppose that was enough.

Only a chief understood what a chief went through, I guess.

"Once we're back topside," I announced before we returned, "we need to be very careful about what we say and do. I don't believe Lydia is able to hear us, but it's possible. I also don't know whether or not she feeds information to the Directors about the things we say, but, again, it's possible."

"Never did trust her," Rachel spat.

"She's not real, Rachel," I pointed out. "She can only do what her programming allows." That gave me an idea. "I wonder if Turbo can check things out and see if we're being tapped or not? I'll have to have a word with him."

We all grabbed hands again and I gave a nod to Valerie, signaling that we were ready to go.

She winked in return and blew me a kiss.

Rachel seemed to enjoy that.

I sighed as the valkyries and Lucy faded from view.

## CHAPTER 24

*W*e arrived back in the garage at Caesar's Palace. As soon as we appeared, I activated my connector and called back to base while holding up my finger to signal everyone else to be quiet.

*"Lydia, have there been any additional reports about crazy stuff going on?"*

*"Nothing yet, sugar plum,"* she replied. *"I was a bit worried there because you and the entire team disappeared."*

*"Ah...we had to go to the lowest levels here at Caesar's. Just came back up."* I hesitated but figured I'd use her concern as an opportunity to ask how much she kept tabs on us. *"Are you always able to hear what we say, baby?"*

*"Oh, no,"* she replied as if shocked I would ask such a thing. *"That would go against privacy protocols. But I can and do keep track of your whereabouts at all times. That's a requirement, puddin'."*

*"And probably a good one,"* I admitted, but decided to

press the point further. *"So when I'm having a discussion with Rachel about personal matters, you don't listen in on that?"*

*"Definitely not. Why would I want to do that?"*

She sounded miffed. This probably had more to do with the fact that I was in a relationship with Rachel than with Lydia feeling as though I was accusing her of something, though. It was clear that she was jealous of Rachel and me getting back together.

I cracked a smile at that.

*"Now, don't be that way, my little digital delicacy,"* I teased as Rachel rolled her eyes. *"You know I didn't mean anything negative."*

*"I like that nickname,"* Lydia said after a moment.

*"It's fitting, don't you think?"*

She did a little digital giggle. *"Yes."*

*"Anyway, I have heard things about those systems that can overhear what you say. You know, like that one from Amaz—"*

*"Ian,"* Lydia interrupted hotly, *"if you dare compare me to that lowly piece of technology, we're going to have a serious problem."*

I damn near laughed out loud at that. Only I could manage to piss off an artificial intelligence dispatcher.

*"I wouldn't dream of it,"* I breathed, acting my best to sound dreadful. *"I merely meant that those inferior units listen in even when they're not being actively questioned."* I let that sink in for a moment. *"The only way I could compare you to them is if you listened in all the time. But as you've clearly pointed out, you're far superior to those, so you wouldn't do such a thing."*

There was the slightest hesitation, which meant that Lydia was processing what I'd just said. She was wicked fast, so any delay at all signaled logic relays were working overtime.

"*Correct,*" she said finally.

And now it was time to do a little damage control. I had to keep her on my side as best as possible. While the Directors may have her in their pocket from a power standpoint, my hope was that she'd stand with me on the side of loyalty. Not likely being that she was A.I., but she *did* fancy me.

"*Besides,*" I said in a seductive whisper, "*one of these days you'll be given a physical form. When that day comes, you and I are going to be doing the horizontal dance all night.*"

"Ugh," said Rachel, but she knew I was just playing the game.

"*That would be a dream come true,*" admitted Lydia, sounding like she may be on the mend.

"*For me too, baby.*"

Another digital giggle came through.

$\mathcal{I}$ still wasn't one hundred percent sure about Lydia, but I also couldn't expect the team to function without using our connectors. There was simply too much coordination that needed to be done. Besides, I had the feeling that just speaking aloud wouldn't block her from hearing us anyway, assuming she could hear us without our starting an active connection. I know she said she wouldn't, but something told me the Directors had her hanging on our every word. Hopefully my suggesting there was inferior technology out there that had no choice but to listen in uninvited was messing with her logic pathways, at least.

It all came down to trust.

Unfortunately, there wasn't a great track record with the Directors since the ubers showed up.

As we padded back to our cars, Felicia asked what the plan was.

"We're going to go and talk to the owners of the Djinn

Ink Club," I said. "It seems to me that we have a vampire who promised a djinn special powers if he put me in a trance. We all know how touchy the djinn get over anything that may put them in a bad light topside, so they might help."

"Good point," agreed Rachel.

"The vampire community isn't exactly fond of the reputation we have either," Chuck pointed out. "Everyone just assumes that if you're a vampire, you must be some kind of narcissist."

To be fair, the majority of vampires were exactly that. There were many who acted mostly normal, but few vampires were like Chuck. He was as laidback a vampire as you'd likely meet. Well, unless he was kicking your ass all over the place because you'd done something nefarious, of course.

"I'm sure the djinn are going to be unhappy with what Sylvester has done," I said, "but hopefully they won't blame all vampires for it."

They would.

Even though there had been a lot of growth over the years in the realm of racial tension, the different factions still harbored distrust and distaste for one another at the more affluent levels. Old money, as they called it. It was definitely better topside, but it still wasn't perfect. I remember dealing with it during my year as a junior officer in the Netherworld. Within the Netherworld's hub city people *tried* to get along, but if a vampire got too close to the djinn's main area...lights out, brother. Same for a pixie flying into the fae area. Where the city center was a melting pot of turbulence, the edges of town were essentially gangs. Refined gangs, but still quite deadly.

Again, it *was* better up here because different races couldn't easily build those same gang areas. A few would pop up now and then, but one call to the Netherworld PPD would put Retrievers on their tails. Getting and staying topside was tough, and people weren't fond of being forced back for deep reintegration, so most learned to push past their prejudice and try to work in harmony.

I personally had no major issues with any particular class of supernatural. This probably had to do with the fact that I contained all of them in my genetic code. But, I *did* have issues with people who went after others simply because they were born into a different class.

Ignorance I could deal with; stupidity, not so much.

Now, to be fair, I *did* hate it when people assumed I was a vampire. But this had nothing to do with my disliking vampires because they were vampires. It had to do with the fact that nobody ever made the assumption I was a fae or a werewolf or a werebear. That meant their determination was based solely on the fact that I dressed nice and combed my hair…and that I appeared arrogant.

Okay, so sue me, but vampires are notorious for being arrogant.

They knew it.

Hell, they're proud of it!

That's why it bugged me when people singled me out as being a vampire. I had a healthy ego, but I wasn't a pompous ass.

Everyone hopped in their cars and headed off to the Djinn Ink Club. It was located in the same strip mall where I'd been attacked while trying to get the Big Ass Burrito I never got. In that little shopping center was a hidden area that ran underneath the Exotic Cars Vegas rental agency.

"Do you think they'll help?" asked Rachel, referring to the djinn.

"I do, actually."

"Why?"

"Because it's in their best interest. They've been very particular about doing everything by the book ever since the 2013 Dream Scare at Halloween."

I saw her nodding out of the corner of my eye.

"That was pretty bad."

At first, we'd thought it had just been a bunch of people doing a flashmob thing where they all walked around in various costumes acting crazed. But when folks started falling down in the streets, nearly getting killed by cars and causing all sorts of traffic jams, we started to think there was more to it than an organized prank. It had turned out that a set of djinn had become disgruntled and thus took it upon themselves to wreak havoc on the Strip. They'd picked the perfect time to do it because everyone was dressed up and trick-or-treating. Anyway, that landed those djinn in the slammer for a long time with loads of deep reintegration. It also put the djinn community under the watchful eye of the PPD. They *did* have the unique ability to fuck with people's minds, after all. Wizards could do it too, of course, but not with a simple touch.

Vampires had the ability to inject venom and build slaves, which was kind of the same thing, but even those slaves had enough sense not to kill themselves. Give their lives to protect their master? Sure. But they still had most of their wits about them.

"Yeah," I agreed with Rachel. "It took the djinn community a few years to recover. I don't think that they'd want to go through something like that again, which means they'll do whatever they have to in order to exonerate themselves in this incident."

"Assuming they're not involved," she pointed out.

I looked at her.

"You never know," she said.

Hadn't thought of that.

## CHAPTER 26

The moment we parked, a crushing force rocked my Aston Martin.

I'd thought for certain that another vehicle had struck us, but when we got knocked around again, I looked out to see that there was a werewolf standing there.

He howled.

"What the shit?" I said.

"Must be another of the vampire's toys for you," Rachel said. "What say you just shoot this one and be done with it?"

She was probably right, but with all the pent-up aggression I had floating through my system, using Boomy just seemed trite.

"Nah," I said, "I think I'll do it the old-fashioned way."

I stepped out of the car as my opponent backed away. He was giving me a moment to get set.

That was nice.

"You're dead," he growled in a way that only

werewolves could. "I'll rip you to shreds and then I'll feast on that little slut you have with you."

"Excuse me?" Rachel stormed. "Did you call me a slut?"

"Yep."

"Let me tell you something—"

"Technically," I chimed in, coming to the wolf's defense, "you *do* want me to bone a bunch of valkyries while you watch."

"Which makes *you* the slut," she pointed out.

I nodded my agreement. "What does it make you, then?"

"I'd go with awesome," the wolf answered before Rachel could. Then he turned to her and said, "Sorry about the slut comment. What say after I kill this jerk-off, you and I get together? I don't have any problem with you watching me bone other chicks."

"I may take you up on that," Rachel hissed and then gave me a dark look.

"Nice."

I took off my jacket and holster, setting them both on the hood of my car. Then I loosened my tie a bit and undid the top buttons on my shirt. Finally, I rolled up my sleeves and prepared to brawl.

To his credit, the wolf allowed me a little time to prepare, though he did howl twice more while waiting.

He wasn't quite the uber wolf that Rex had been back in London, but this guy was still pretty big. My worry was not knowing the kind of perks Sylvester had given him, assuming this guy *was* given something by the blasted vampire.

"Quick question before we start," I said while

stretching. "Did Sly enhance you in some way in exchange for killing me?"

The wolf furrowed his brow. "Who's Sly?"

"Sylvester Melbourne," I answered. "The vampire?"

"Oh, right. Yeah, gave me really powerful jaws." He then tilted his head. "By the way, I don't think he likes being called Sly."

"How do you know?" I asked. "You weren't even sure who I was referring to when I called him Sly."

"Yeah, but one of his minions called him 'Silly Sylvester' and he killed the guy."

"Well, that's not really the same thing, now is it?"

Clearly, Sly didn't enhance this guy's brain because he looked to be genuinely weighing my question.

"I guess not," he admitted finally.

"One more thing," I said before the games began. "How'd you know we were going to be here?"

He sighed, clearly wanting to get on with things.

"Sylvester said you'd likely be coming back to the scene of the original encounter. He said I had to wait here for you." He then looked at his wrist, which did *not* contain a watch, and added, "Might I say that it took you long enough? I have things to do, you know? The world does not revolve around you."

"Right."

The rest of my team started to arrive. They clearly saw my predicament, but they'd known me long enough to realize when it was best not to interfere. Unless, of course, I started to lose very badly. Then they would definitely come to my rescue. You may find that dishonorable, but when it comes to me dying while a bad guy lives, fuck honor.

"I'm quite a good fighter," I boasted. "Are you ready to die?"

His teeth flared an instant before he launched at me.

Knowing that his jaws were the primary thing to worry about, I ducked under and drove my fist into his gut. He grunted with the impact but landed on all fours and spun back for another attack.

He was damn fast, but I was faster.

I dodged his second attack and brought up my foot to tag the side of his head.

It felt like I'd kicked iron.

Sly obviously *did* put some special sauce into this doggy's jaw. Yes, I realize that sounded dirty.

Before I had a chance to bring my foot back down, Snuggles the Wonder Pup had turned his head just enough to lock on to the heel of my shoe. He yanked it free from my foot and tore into it like it was a perfectly seared filet mignon topped with black truffles. I'd gotten used to the fact that my shoes were one of the first things to get destroyed on this job, but this fuck nut just shredded one of my black Testoni Derby Caps. Not only were these shoes expensive, they were incredibly comfortable.

That's when the pixie came to life.

"Look what you did, you inbred cock-sniffer!"

He paused and looked at me with shock on his face.

I stepped over and ripped the shoe from his mouth and held it up to his face.

"Do you have any idea how much I love this shoe, cum burper?"

"Uh…"

"While I'm sure you are fond of your…" I paused to look down at his feet. His morphed feet had basically ripped his shoes to shreds, signaling he couldn't afford magically altered ones. "No names, I'm guessing?"

"Uh…"

"Picked them up at a thrift shop, no doubt?"

He swallowed, looking hurt. "No reason to be mean about it."

"This shoe," I raged on, shaking the torn Testoni in his face, "could buy a hundred of the ones you're wearing, you stupid labia muppet."

That's when he stood tall and crossed his arms, glaring at me.

"You spent that much on a pair of shoes?" he said with a laugh. "Who is the idiot in this situation again?"

"You are," I spat, throwing the shoe at his head. "Ass fiddler."

He roared and grabbed my shoulders quicker than I'd expected. Fortunately, I'd tilted my head away just enough to avoid him decapitating me. Unfortunately, it wasn't enough to stop him from chomping into my shoulder.

To say that it hurt would be understating things. Imagine being the guinea pig patient for the very first do-it-yourself-at-home-vasectomy-kit, and you'd get the gist of the anguish that bite caused.

But that just helped to bring the magic out again.

My right hand unleashed a flow of energy daggers in rapid succession. They blew right through Snuggles so quickly that he was literally halved within seconds. But I was so charged up that the electric blades continued flying from my hand and off into the night. They slowly dissipated before falling back to the ground, though, so at least nobody would be injured by them.

Rachel rushed over and grabbed my arm.

"Ian," she yelled, barely breaking through my angst, "calm down! He's dead already!"

Felicia and Chuck were on the other side of me, working to dislodge Snuggles' jaw from my shoulder. Serena was standing by to apply her healing hands.

Slowly, I regained control of myself and the magic stopped.

"Fucker shouldn't have destroyed my shoes," I mumbled, feeling incredibly tired as my crew got the wolf dislodged from my shoulder and dropped him to the ground. He turned back into a human. "Fucking cock-juggling snatch cave."

Serena's hands went to work on me. Coupled with my own healing ability, my shoulder was back to normal within a few minutes. But I was still exhausted.

Casting magic was a tiring business.

"I'm going to need you guys to funnel some of your power into me," I said tiredly as I looked toward the building where the Djinn Ink Club was housed. "I can't go in there feeling this weak."

The mages all nodded and put their hands on me.

"Oooh," I said without control. "That feels amazing."

CHAPTER 27

*J*decided that it might be best if my team stayed outside to make sure we weren't ambushed when we exited. We could still be attacked, obviously, but with the crew outside we'd at least have shields in place. Plus, we'd be entrenched instead of walking out blind.

Thus, after putting my suit jacket back on and grabbing a fresh pair of shoes from the trunk of my Aston Martin, Rachel and I entered the door past the hidden area.

The place was posh, with comfortable carpeting, dark blue walls that were dimly lit via sconces, and furniture that looked very cozy. All of this made sense seeing that the point was to make you feel like you were in a calm place. Most of the people who frequented the joint were normals, after all, so to them this would be the perfect environment for dreaming. The normals who came here were typically wealthy, but not always. Regardless, they couldn't get in unless they were in-the-know. First off, there was a hidden zone; secondly, there was a null zone. Any normal without the proper training and bypass protocols wouldn't even know the Djinn Ink Club existed.

Rachel and I sauntered up to the main desk where there stood a muscular djinn dude. He had tattoos running up his neck, ending along his jawline. It looked kind of like a dark turtleneck sweater.

"What can we do for you two today?" he asked in a voice that sounded like it belonged to a much smaller man. "Lovers paradise, maybe? We've got a sale going on for that one. Twenty-five hundred each." He winked. "That's a bargain, too. One hour of sensual bliss. Multiple orgasms, orgies, and essentially any desire fulfilled that you can imagine."

"We'll take it," Rachel blurted.

I shook my head and frowned at her. "What? No, we won't. We're on the job, remember?"

"Huh?" she replied, blinking at me. "Oh, right. Sorry."

Seriously, this role-reversal thing was getting a little out of hand. And I honestly didn't understand it anyway. I mean, I knew why *I* was acting differently, but what was her deal? She seemed to dig the fact that I was being more demanding, edgy, and riddled with angst, but even when I wasn't being that way it was like her horny meter was up.

"Right," I said, taking out my badge and showing it to Muscles Mitch. "We'd like to speak to the elders, please."

His demeanor changed into one that was a bit more dark.

"What's this about?"

"Are you an elder?" I asked, knowing for certain that he was not.

"No."

"Then it's none of your concern."

He sneered at me. I didn't flinch in the slightest. Muscles or not, all it would take was for me to get behind him and I'd tear his ass apart. Again, I realize that sounded wrong.

"Wait here," he commanded.

I glanced around. "Where else would we go?"

That seemed to confuse the poor fellow. He merely stormed off and went through a back room, hopefully on his way to fetch someone from the elders. If they were involved, though, it could be that he was just snagging some backup.

Just in case, I put my hand on Boomy.

"Be ready for anything, Rachel," I whispered. "Hopefully this will be peaceful but, as you noted earlier, these guys might be part of the problem."

Her eyes dulled slightly, which let me know she was preparing herself for a fight. She sometimes did this, or went into a full trance, right before going into a shady situation. It was either that or her hands started glowing. Obviously, she considered that might be construed by the djinn as a direct act of aggression.

I scanned the place and found a number of normals relaxing next to djinn. They all looked to be feeling rather peaceful. That made sense seeing that they were likely experiencing one amazing dream.

Those dreams were pricey, though.

Hell, I would argue that a crack habit would be less taxing on the wallet than a djinn dream addiction. The primary difference was that djinn dreams weren't likely to kill you or mess with your brain chemistry. In other words, they didn't cause physical addiction like your average street drugs, but rather they built a dependency on the realization that reality sucked in comparison. Spending an hour on the beach getting blown by ten supermodels was far better than sitting at your crap job doing reports that you couldn't give two shits about... speaking from a guy's perspective, anyway.

Just as Rachel's eyes cleared, Muscles Mitch came back out of the back room and waved us over.

"No funny stuff," he said with a hint of menace, "and hand me your weapons."

"No," I replied without inflection.

He crossed his massive arms and glared at me.

"Then you can't go back there."

"We're officers from the Paranormal Police Department," I countered. "Unlike standard officers, we do not need a search warrant to enter *any* building or area of *any* building that is run or frequented by supernaturals." I tilted my head and looked up at him. "This isn't the Netherworld, Mitch."

He grimaced. "Who's Mitch?"

"Oh, uh…" I coughed. "Sorry, what was your name again?"

"Milton."

Muscles Milton worked as well as Muscles Mitch.

"Right. Sorry." I peered over at Rachel, who had that determined look of a mage who was ready for action. "Anyway, this is the Overworld. The rules are different here, and you should know that."

"Yeah, yeah," he said with a grunt. "I *do* know that, but I don't see any reason for you bringing your weapons back there unless you plan to start trouble."

"I promise you that *we* won't start anything," I replied, though it was unnecessary. He had no way to stop me, aside from using force, but that would be a bad move on his part...even if he didn't know it. "It's in the best interest of everyone here that we make this as smooth as possible, so what say you move out of our way and go pump yourself or something?"

He bridled at that remark.

When the pixie in my genetic code wanted to speak, I had to put all my focus on shutting him up; otherwise, he would just blabber on as if I'd been inflicted with Tourette's. At least my language hadn't been filthy this time.

With a scowl, Milton stepped aside.

## CHAPTER 28

The back room wasn't as dark and calming. In fact, it kind of felt like we had walked into a standard office conference room, minus the windows. The table was made of white stone with flecks of metal embedded in it. And the chairs were all the high-back, leather, top-of-the-line models.

This was my kind of place.

At the head of the table sat Elaine Kouross, the current leader of the Vegas Djinn. We'd met on a number of occasions over the years. Of course I'd met with all the heads of the various factions in town. It was part of my job. The only ones I didn't have to schedule a day each year for were the Directors, but that's only because I saw them quite often already.

To her left was Ted Preston and to her right sat Glenn Clifford. They were her vice chairmen. Suck-ups, mostly. Each one looking to be her replacement when the time came. Every five years, each faction was required to go through an election phase. Elaine had won the last three elections in a landslide.

She was calm, cool, and seemed to genuinely care about her people.

"Chief Dex," she said, motioning for me and Rachel to take a seat, "to what do we owe the pleasure of your visit tonight?"

So she was going to play this aloof.

That put me on edge, frankly.

Again, I'd dealt with Elaine more than once and while she was always distant during our discussions, she never came across as being in league with the criminal element. Even when the Halloween fiasco happened, she had been exceedingly helpful in doing all she could to make sure things got resolved smoothly. Of course, that *had* been an election year.

Still, I'd never known her to be...

I glanced at her for a moment. Maybe Sylvester had gotten to her as well? Maybe he'd gotten to all of them?

That was a dreadful thought.

"I'm sure you heard about the djinn who attacked me earlier?"

Her eyes flashed slightly.

"No," she said, leaning forward and looking genuinely concerned. "What are you talking about?"

"I was taking a stroll to get a Big Ass Burrito over at Tommy Rocker's—"

"Love those things," Glenn interrupted. "Sorry."

I nodded at him and gave a fake smile. "Anyway, just as I walked onto the parking lot, one of your djinn started trying to sell me on getting a dream."

"There's no law against that," Elaine noted.

"No, there isn't," I agreed, "but you may well recall that I'm an amalgamite, which means that your particular skills don't work on me."

"Yes, we know."

"Well, when your employee touched my arm, I started hallucinating."

Her eyes studied me for a moment. She seemed quite interested in the fact that someone from her group had managed to break my mental wall after all these years.

"Go on," she said, looking amused.

"He'd had the help of someone else," I stated coolly. "A vampire."

All three of them looked like they'd suddenly been slapped.

"That's right," I said, nodding at them. "He's been going around giving enhanced powers to any sucker who will agree to assassinate me. So far we have captured a goblin mage, killed a werebear, killed a werewolf, and killed your former employee."

"You killed him?"

"Kill or be killed, I'm afraid," I answered. "He put me into a hallucinated state so that the vampire could bite me. After that, I kind of lost my mind and ripped your guy's throat out."

Elaine's jaw fell slack as her face contorted into a look of horror. She was clearly not pleased to hear my news. Neither were the other two.

"Now," I said before they could respond, "I'm hoping that none of you had anything to do with this, but I had to speak with you to make certain."

She swallowed hard, obviously recalling how fragile the djinn's community presence was on the Strip. There was no way that Elaine had any desire to go through another scandal.

"We will review all records," she stated quickly while snapping her fingers at Ted. He ran out. "We'll also check all video feeds and do interviews with every employee." Glenn took off. "I can assure you that there was no coordinated event that I'm aware of, but if anything untoward has happened, I'll find out about it."

I nodded slowly.

"I believe you," I said, though the jury was still out, if I was being honest. "We're looking for the vampire, too. My guess is he came in here and got with the djinn who attacked me."

"Do you know a name?" she asked as she took out her data pad.

"Sylvester Melbourne," I answered.

"Sorry, I meant the name of the djinn who *allegedly* attacked you."

"Ah," I replied, ignoring the 'allegedly' comment. "I don't, but if you have employee photos, I'd be happy to take a look through them."

"Or you could just see which one of your workers is missing," suggested Rachel in a monotone voice.

She was still in her dazed state.

"True," I agreed.

Elaine pushed herself up and walked to the door. She paused for a moment and then turned back to look at us.

"Actually," she said as she motioned us to join her, "let's do both."

## CHAPTER 29

The djinn who had attacked me was Rip Lewis. He was only six months topside. It was unfortunate that he'd drawn the straw that landed him with Sylvester as a client. Then again, the promise of the easy way was always wrought with trials. I'd learned long ago that there really wasn't such a thing as shortcuts, unless you were very lucky.

"We have video, Ms. Kouross," announced Glenn as he and Ted entered the room. "We also have a scarf."

"A scarf?" I asked with a raised eyebrow.

"Yes, sir," Ted answered. "We saw on the video that he'd checked it in at the front desk, but he was in such a hurry to leave that he never picked it back up."

Ted set the scarf down beside me. It was a dark red color that no doubt matched Sylvester's favorite drink. I picked it up and looked at it, when the scent of it hit me like a sledgehammer.

I pointed at the video and said, "We don't need that."

Rachel looked at me, coming down from her mage high. "What?"

"I have Sylvester's scent," I whispered, holding the scarf. "Between Felicia and me, we can track the guy."

"Ah, right." Rachel stood up, her nose scrunched up like she'd just been around someone the day after they'd eaten a Big Ass Burrito. "Forgot about the wolf thing."

That seemed a bit odd. So she was cool with the vampire fangs and all that, but wasn't into me also being a werewolf? I knew she was more of a cat person, but this was a bit different.

Whatever.

"Where are you going?" asked Elaine as we started for the door.

"I can track the guy with this…" I realized what I was saying and coughed. "I mean *we* can…one of my officers is a werewolf. *She* can track Sylvester by using his scent on the scarf."

"I see," she said, nodding. "We're going with you."

"What?"

"I said—"

"I heard what you said," I interrupted, "but it's out of the question."

"Why?"

"Because this a police matter, not an avenue for you to act out a vendetta." I noticed the look of determination on her face. "I'm serious, Elaine…Ms. Kouross." I didn't want to act too informal around her executives. "The fact is that there's bound to be a violent clash when we get to Sylvester, and I have little doubt that he's turned more than just the few we've already run into. If you're there, that's just one more set of people that we'll have to watch."

She put her hand on her hip and started wagging a finger in my face. I hated it when women did that to me, and it happened more often than I cared to remember.

"Listen to me, Chief Dex," she snarled, "that damnable vampire has turned one of my people. He twisted that poor boy's mind and got him killed. For all we know, he may have turned even more of my people." Her eyes were firm, which looked really freaky next to all the ink that was etched on her face. "If you think I'm going to sit idly by in the hopes that your crew can bring this bastard to justice, you've got another thing coming."

I understood her point. Really, I did. But the fact was that I couldn't be responsible for them. My crew was trained for this sort of thing. Her folks weren't. They were trained to attack and kill, sure. That came with growing up in the Netherworld. But this was different.

"I'm sorry, Ms. Kouross," I stated firmly, "but no." She went to speak but I held up my hand. "If you get involved, I'll have you and everyone you bring along arrested. I will also recommend deep reintegration for each of you."

She did *not* look happy.

"We'll get him," Rachel assured her, her eyes nearly clear again. "I promise you that we'll get him."

With that, we headed back out of the building and got ready for the hunt.

## CHAPTER 30

Warren and Serena had headed back to the precinct in order to work on their findings with the werebear I'd killed at Caesar's. They'd also had some samples from the werewolf I'd destroyed here. I wasn't sure what Serena had in mind, but she seemed hellbent on doing whatever she could to help the vampires that Sylvester likely had under his venomous spell. Warren just seemed to want to avoid fighting.

Felicia and I compared notes on the scent of Sylvester's scarf. It was an odd sensation to track things via smell. I'd almost say it was like *seeing* the line of odor.

"You're kidding me," I said as I stared off at the building that the scent appeared to end at. I sniffed the air again. "I'll be damned."

"Is that a problem?" asked Felicia, staring in the same direction I was. "If anything, it'll make our ability to track him even simpler."

"Not a problem, no," I replied. "Just an incredible coincidence."

I walked back to the rest of my crew and found Rachel was giving everyone the lowdown on what had happened with the djinn. She seemed to be back to normal again.

Well, normal was a relative term, I suppose.

Prior to my getting bitten by Sylvester, her normal disposition was snarky and somewhat bossy; since the bite, she was more lovey and, well, melty. It was like she was swooning and such. I preferred Rachel to be swoonless. I wasn't a fan of the swoon.

"It seems our vampire pal has made a home of it at Tommy Rocker's," I announced.

"The place you were going when you were attacked?" Rachel asked.

"One and the same, yes." I glanced back over and sighed. "There's no doubt going to be a null and hidden zone over there. Probably around back." I had the urge to smell the air again. "Yep, definitely around back."

We started walking as my mages prepared themselves for a showdown. Chuck and Felicia had their guns out, checking to make sure everything was set. I had a feeling I wouldn't need Boomy, but one could never be too careful when it came to showdowns.

Just as we crossed under the far covered-parking section, Felicia abruptly stopped.

I sensed something was amiss too, but I was *trying* not to be too werewolfy. Rachel apparently wasn't fond of that element in my genetic code. Not that it was my fault. It wasn't like I'd chosen the bits of DNA that filled my personage. Did I complain that she was incapable of ordering her own dessert at a restaurant while simultaneously being *fully* capable of devouring whichever one I ordered? No. To be fair, that seemed to be what chicks did in general.

Regardless, I accepted her faults.

I reflexively glanced at her in fear that she may have sensed my thoughts.

She didn't.

I felt instantly ashamed.

Here I was, a major badass with powers that were insane, but I was still terrified of my girlfriend. Sometimes I wondered if I even deserved testicles.

"Wait," I whispered, sniffing the air again. "Shit."

"You smell that, too?" asked Felicia.

Jasmine frowned at us. "You guys smell shit?"

"Huh?" Felicia and I responded in unison.

Then, I grunted.

"No, I was just using an expletive." I motioned everyone to move to the other side of a red van that was parked next to us. "There are a couple of people over there." I was pointing at the back corner of Tommy Rocker's. "They have Sylvester's scent on them."

"Sentries," Griff noted. "There are likely more in the area."

Both Felicia and I began sniffing around.

Literally.

Sure enough, one was just around the edge of A Touch of Las Vegas Day Spa and Salon.

"Stay low," I said as the guy turned and began walking

along the building. He turned left at the corner and continued on into the back parking area where deliveries came in. "I have an idea. We need to get a djinn to help us, though."

"Yikes," said Rachel.

## CHAPTER 31

*I* rushed into the Djinn Ink Club and raced through to the back where Elaine, Ted, and Glenn were located. Muscles Milton had chased after me but was dismissed with a flick of Elaine's wrist. He did not look pleased about that.

Tough shit.

"What is it?" Elaine asked.

"We've found Sylvester's hideout," I explained, "and he's got sentries roaming the area. I was hoping I could get you or one of your people to help us extract information from them. He should be out back of this building right now."

Elaine didn't even hesitate. She took a brisk walk through the various cubicles along the back of the office, stepped out into the night air but stayed inside of the hidden zone that protected the exit from being seen.

"That him?" she whispered as we watched the guy I'd seen earlier clomping past.

He could see into a null zone, just like any super, but even super's eyes couldn't penetrate a hidden zone unless there was magic involved.

"Yes," I answered, sniffing the air once more just in case. "He may be able to contact his base, though, so we have—"

Elaine put her finger to her lips and then motioned me to stay put.

She walked out of the zone in the opposite direction that the sentry was moving, clearly wanting to ensure he didn't just see her blink into existence. That would have jarred him, for sure.

After a few steps, she turned around, looked at the man's back, rolled her eyes, and then proceeded to fall down.

"Ouch," she yelped, acting as though she were injured.

The guy jumped and spun around, looking ready to pounce. Then he saw Elaine on the ground and rushed over to help her.

Honestly, I wasn't expecting that.

"Are you okay, lady?" he asked as he helped her to her feet. "It's like you came out of nowhere."

"Oh," she replied, feigning lightheadedness. "I was just leaving the shop through that door there," she pointed, "and I guess I stepped wrong or something."

The poor guy looked quite concerned for her well-being. That made me kind of feel bad because I had the sneaking suspicion that he was going to be pushing up daisies soon. This is what happened when you played for the bad guys, though. Of course it also happened when you played for the good guys, but thankfully not as often.

"Is there anything I can do?" he asked. "Maybe I can help you to your car?"

"That would be lovely," she replied as she put her hand on his neck.

He slumped almost instantly as Elaine stood up straight, stopping the pain act and regaining her composure.

"He's out," she announced. "Let's get him inside and see what he knows."

"That was fast," I replied, grabbing the guy by his arm and leading him toward the door. His face resembled what I remembered those zombies from months ago looking like. Zoned out. "I thought it took a little while to put people at your mercy?"

"It does," she stated, "but he was already halfway there. That's why I played the damsel-in-distress card. His mind was already sympathetic toward me. He was emotionally attached to the fact that I was injured, as it were. If he'd have been an asshole, it wouldn't have worked. Fortunately, he wasn't."

I gave her an appraising look. "Clever."

"You learn a thing or two when you've been doing this for as long as I have."

We got him into the building and lowered him onto one of the leather chairs in Elaine's office.

She pulled up another chair and put her hands on his face in such a way that made me think of how that Spock guy from *Star Trek* used to do that to people when he was reading thoughts and whatnot. I couldn't help but wonder if maybe the show's creators got the idea for those little hand gestures from the djinn of yesteryear.

"Where is your master?" Elaine whispered.

"Hidden zone behind Tommy Rocker's," the guy answered in a voice laced with bliss. "Beside the tree. There is an access panel that leads underground."

"Why that particular restaurant?"

"The boss loves Big Ass Burritos."

Elaine glanced over at me with a raised eyebrow.

"What?" I said. "They *are* good."

She turned back to him. "How many others has your boss infected?"

"We have an army of nearly fifty," the guy replied proudly. "We cannot be stopped."

"What's the plan for this army?"

He jolted slightly. "I don't know."

"You can tell me."

"I don't know," he said again, this time with more of an edge. "The boss says that underlings are not told these sorts of things."

If Sylvester made it out of this unscathed, maybe he could put in for a position with the Directors. They subscribed to that same leadership mentality, after all.

I went to speak, but Elaine gave me a sharp look and pointed at the whiteboard.

"*How many sentries are there?*" I wrote. "*And where are their positions?*"

She asked him.

"Just three of us," he answered. "My route was to go around the shopping center, keeping an eye out for Officer Ian Dex until the werewolf killed him. The other two are standing near the entrance to the secret area."

Fortunately, the guy's eyes were dulled over or he

would have recognized me immediately. He was staring in my general direction. I had no idea if he would have sent word back to Sylvester at that moment or not, but I decided to turn my head slightly, just in case.

*"Did the werewolf kill Officer Dex?"* I wrote as my next question.

Again, Elaine asked it for me.

"I don't know," he answered, looking anxious. "After checking on the werewolf, I had to use the facilities. When I came back out, the werewolf was gone."

I then wrote, *"Can you make him think I'm dead?"*

Elaine started to ask him that, but I waved her to stop. She gave me a what-the-fuck? look. I replied with a stern grimace and erased what I'd written originally.

*"I'm asking if* you *can make* him *think the werewolf has already killed me so Sylvester won't expect my arrival."*

"Ahhh," she mouthed. "Sorry."

Then she slightly moved her fingers around on the guy's face. His brow creased. If I had to guess, I'd say that this new finger layout put him in a bit of pain.

"You *did* see the fight," Elaine instructed him. "The werewolf beat Officer Dex and devoured his head. The wolf also urinated and defecated on the body and threw it into the garbage."

*"What the fuck?"* I wrote on the board. *"That's disgusting."*

"It's believable," she sassed with a whisper. "Deal with it."

"It's believable," repeated the guy. "I'll deal with it."

Elaine winced and turned back to the dude, obviously recognizing that she had spoken when she shouldn't have.

I stuck my tongue out at her.

"You will go back to your boss and tell him that Officer Dex is dead," she commanded. "Do you understand?"

"I understand," he answered.

She removed her fingers and his head lulled. He still wasn't out, but he looked to have seen better days.

"He's done," she said. "Let's get him out of here."

We then got him to his feet and back out to the parking lot. As soon as Elaine was in generally the same position as she was before she'd put him under her spell earlier, she brought him back to reality.

"My goodness," she said as the guy looked around, seemingly confused. "You know, I think I'll be okay."

"Yeah?" he said, clearly baffled and disoriented. "Are… are you sure?"

"Yes. Thank you *so much* for being a gentleman."

He blinked a few times and shook his head.

"No problem, ma'am," he said. "No problem at all."

# CHAPTER 32

*A*fter leaving the Djinn Ink Club and waiting for the duped sentry to disappear around the edge of the building, we high-tailed it toward Tommy Rocker's.

Although we couldn't see the sentries due to the hidden zone, Felicia and I could smell them just fine.

"You take the one on the left and I'll get the one on the right," I said.

"Do you really have to kill them, Chief?" Chuck asked. "It's not their fault that Sylvester put them under a spell."

I held Boomy in check and looked at him.

"I know this sucks, Chuck," I said as gently as I could, "but we have to stop this guy. His victims are not capable of highly rational thought at the moment, right?"

He sighed and looked down. "Right."

"Listen," I whispered, "if you want to head back to the station, I'll understand."

"I'm a cop, Chief," he replied. "I don't walk away just because things get inconvenient."

"Right."

Felicia and I lifted our guns and dropped the two sentries. The one thing about breaker bullets was that they did the job every time, assuming you hit near the heart, at least. This was especially true with the new style of bullet that Turbo had created, having wood, silver, and magical elements all built in.

We rushed over and entered the hidden area. The two bodies were just empty shells now, but I could still see the angst on Chuck's face as Griff put a hand on his shoulder. We moved the bodies to sit up against the side wall, which gave them a little bit of respectability.

"Sorry, Chuck."

"I know."

Felicia had pulled open the hatch and we saw a wide set of stairs leading down to a concrete floor.

Just as Felicia went to take the first step, I pulled her back and pointed. She looked, but she clearly didn't see anything.

I scanned the faces of the mages, too.

Nothing.

"You guys can't see those runes?"

Rachel cast a quick spell that dropped a dust-like magical cloud over the area. This sufficed in making the runes glitter.

"Those are—" Rachel started.

"Notification, shock, and entanglement runes," I interrupted. "Yes, I know. I don't suppose any of you can undo them?"

Rachel and Jasmine shook their heads. Griff, however,

was rubbing his goatee thoughtfully. He turned his head this way and that as if studying them.

"Griff?" I questioned.

"I believe I can, but it may take some time. Probably fifteen minutes or so."

"I don't think that'll work," I stated and then turned and held my hand out instinctively.

A beam of particles exited my palm and struck the first rune, slowly erasing it in a very precise way. I knew exactly what was happening, which made it all the more strange.

"What are you doing?" croaked Jasmine.

"I'm un-drawing the rune from its end point," I explained. "You have to do it stroke for stroke in reverse from how it was originally drawn for it to work."

The first one was down within a minute. The next two went by even faster.

"Marry me," Rachel cooed with a face of awe.

I squinted at her. "You're acting really strange."

She jolted and blinked.

"Oh, and you're not?" she retaliated, showing a little of that Rachel independence again.

"Touché."

I took the first step and slowly descended the staircase. The last thing I wanted to do was rush things and end up tripping over a rune. Since I clearly had the ability to detect and wipe them out, I was able to set the pace for everyone else.

We reached the bottom of the steps and I heard cheers coming from down the hall.

A quick scan of the area told me that the runes were only placed at the entrance. That was good, at least.

The voices grew louder as we turned down one of the hallways that led to a large set of doors.

I held up my hand and everyone stopped.

"And I have just had word that Officer Ian Dex has been assassinated!" exclaimed a proud voice.

More cheers.

Clearly this was Sylvester doing a rally for his troops.

"With him out of the way," he continued, "we'll be able to take over Las Vegas, and then the world!"

I glanced back as the vampire army cheered again.

My crew's faces were a mixture of hurt and anger. For it to be suggested that *I* was the only one capable of stopping him was asinine.

Sylvester clearly didn't know how good my team was.

Too bad for that fucker, he and his army were about to find out.

## CHAPTER 33

*I* walked up to the double doors that led into the auditorium and stepped inside.

*"Stay back here,"* I said to my team through the connector. *"You'll have the higher ground when the shit hits the fan."*

Nobody argued. They knew there was no point.

Sylvester kept on talking until I got about halfway to the stage.

His voice caught and he looked at me with disbelieving eyes. His followers clearly noted the look on his face because I suddenly felt a bunch of eyes on me. Now that I had their attention, it was time to channel a bit of pixie and rattle his nerves.

"How's it going, Sly?" I called out. "You look a little pale. Of course, that could just be because you're a vampire." Then I pointed to a woman near me. "She looks kind of tan, so I guess that's not it." I snapped my fingers and pointed at him. "Wait, could this be due to the fact that you thought I was dead? I'll bet that's it."

"Did you just call me 'Sly'?" he asked in a sinister tone of voice.

"No good?" I asked.

"No."

"Ah, sorry. Maybe you would prefer something a little more colorful, like, say, Sperm Pancake?"

That jarred him. "What?"

"Hmmm…maybe Turd Aficionado?" I squinted. "I can see you don't like that one either." I rubbed my chin for a moment and then my eyes lit up. "Ah! How about we just go with something simple, like Cunt or Douche?"

The rage on his face was palpable. I found this quite humorous, but one look at my team told me that they weren't fond of me riling up the man who was holding the leash on this crowd.

They had a point.

"Alternately," I said, chewing my lip, "I suppose I could just call you Sylvester. Wouldn't be my first choice, but I know how some people are incapable of taking a joke."

My smile was one of the shit-eating variety.

"Kill them," Sylvester commanded.

The vampires turned toward us, but I held up my hand.

"Wait, wait, wait," I objected. "You haven't even given me the bad-guy speech yet." The vampires paused. "Honestly, how can you expect your followers to take you seriously if you don't stick to the evil overlord basics?"

"I…what?" he said, looking like his brain had suddenly starting throbbing. "What are you talking about?"

"Oh, come on, Sly!" I put my hand to my mouth in faux concern. "Sorry…Sylvester. Everyone knows that the bad guy spills his guts to the good guys before he kills them. It's like page one of the naughty rulebook." I pointed at him. "I'm not talking about the sexual naughty rulebook here, but rather the evil one. Just so you know."

He scanned the crowd and clearly noted that their faces were all turned back to him now. Obviously, they were waiting for his response, which should have been a reiteration to kill us all, but I had the feeling he was actually going to spill his guts.

Gullible.

"So, what's the big plan, you festering testicle?" I asked, crossing my arms. "Something fresh and exciting, like maybe taking over a fast-food chain of restaurants and raising the prices to something exorbitant?"

He grimaced. "Huh?"

"Maybe you're planning to rig hotdog eating contests so that you can get your name into the record books?"

"What the hell are you talking about?" he rasped. "Those things are ridiculous!"

I looked thoughtful for a moment before slowly letting my face sink. Then I dropped my head forward and began shaking it. It was overly dramatic, yes, but I was trying to play him here.

*"Get your magic ready, guys,"* I said through the connector, *"and start planning your attack strategy. Sly's going to blow up at any moment. The madder I get him, the better our chances that he'll overreact."*

"Oh no," I wailed like I was in a Shakespearian play.

"*Please* don't tell me you're planning something incredibly cliché like taking over the town."

"Well..." he started, but then coughed.

"Gah! And here I was thinking that you were a higher class of bad guy, Sly!" I groaned and grabbed at my hair. "For fuck's sake. Do you have any idea how many assholes do the I'm-going-to-take-over-the-town routine? It's so boring!"

"But it's—"

"*Boring*, you pee hole," I interrupted, glaring up at him. "I've been a cop in the Vegas PPD for seven years, Sly. Over that time, I've dealt with everything from petty theft to idiots like you who are planning to take over the town. Now, in that seven years of working on the force, how many of those pimply cornholers do you think have succeeded in taking over the town?"

He opened his mouth and closed it a couple of times as his eyes darted from face to face. It was clear that he was starting to sweat. The fighting would start soon.

"*He's getting close, guys,*" I warned my team. "*I hope you're ready for this.*"

"Uhhh..." Sylvester said, finally, "none?"

"Ding, ding, ding!" I bellowed while clapping. "We *have* a winner!"

He smiled for a split second and then immediately shut it down. Some people were just too easy to fuck with. This probably wasn't the best course of action when the person you were tormenting had your life in their hands, but I was never one to be intimidated by the criminal element.

"Look, Sly," I pressed on, "I'm just saying that if you

really want to be remembered as a guy who tried to do the same shit as every other baddie in the history of the city, go for it. But I'd wager that your legacy would be held in higher esteem in your shit-stained community if you shot for something fresh."

He slowly began to smile as his head nodded.

"You're trying to rile me up," he stated. "I have to admit that it was well on its way to working, too. Sadly, you are dealing with a mind that is far superior to your own."

"Right," I said, nonplussed. "A mind that can't think up anything better than taking over the city." I snorted and turned to the closest set of vampires to me. "I can't believe you're actually following this pig fingerer. Honestly, was there a sale on evil overlords at Walmart or something?" I pointed at Sylvester. "He's clearly from the Fucktard collection."

"That's it," shrieked Sylvester. "Kill them now!"

## CHAPTER 34

*A* set of hands reached for me and my fangs popped out, as did my claws. From the outside, I must have looked like Dracula and Wolverine's love child. I dare not wonder who the mama was in that relationship.

I raked my claws across the nearest neck, which would have killed most things, but not a vampire. Well, not unless I'd done more than slice the guy's flesh, anyway. It would have taken a much deeper cut. But it sufficed to have him clutch his throat and back away.

A hand grabbed my shoulder and yanked me around to find a fist flying in for the kill.

I ducked.

The sound of cracking knuckles against a soft nose perked me up, especially since it was followed by a resounding groan.

This gave me time to launch myself straight up. I brought my palm to connect with the underside of the chick's chin who tried to punch me. Her neck snapped at the force of the blow. She tumbled to the ground.

But that just opened me up for another attack. Searing pain shot through my right bicep as a set of fangs sank deeply in. It hurt like crap, but just as I was about to tear that asshole away, I felt a fist hit the back of my head.

I wanted to call out to my team for help, but the chatter ringing out over the connector made it clear that they, too, had their hands full. A quick glance up their way showed fireballs, energy swirls, and ice barrages.

My initial thought was to get up there and help them out, but they had to deal with their fight and I had to deal with mine. Even if I had tried to get up there, I'd have died before making it halfway.

I decided to stay put and trust that they could handle themselves. They did just fine before I joined the Vegas PPD, so I had no reason to suspect that would change anytime soon.

It became clear pretty quickly that watching my crew's light show only sufficed to make me feel even more woozy.

But this was no time to keel over.

I had vampires to kill.

Digging deep, I pulled forth a round of energy and kicked backwards, sending my one attacker through the air. Then I jabbed my fingers into the eyes of the fucker biting my arm. He screamed and let go, hitting the ground at my feet. I jumped up and came straight down on his head, Bruce Lee style. Contrary to popular belief, crushing a vampire's head is just as effective as putting a wooden spike through the heart.

There was no time to gloat over my handiwork, though. Another vampire cannoned into me from the side, driving me to the ground in the process. When we landed, I continued the roll and she flew off of me and struck the wall headfirst.

She died.

I didn't have time to get back to my feet before another set of vamps were on me. It was all I could do to fend off their blows when I felt another one sink its fangs in my calf.

In case you hadn't already guessed, I screamed.

I gotta tell ya, that shit hurt. Take the worst muscle cramp you've ever had, mix it with two long pointy teeth, and fill the holes with burning venom.

Not fun.

Unfortunately for that dude, it also launched another round of adrenaline through my system.

I brought my other leg over and kicked hard down on the guy's head. He gurgled and there was a snapping sound. Not the neck this time, but rather the fucking thing's teeth. They had broken off in my leg.

"Son of a cunt," I growled as I reached up and knocked the heads together of the two vampires who were trying to punch my lights out. They stopped punching. I kept knocking. "Die, fuckers, die!" I hollered, paraphrasing the title of one of my new favorite poets from the nine levels.

They died.

"*Are you guys okay?*" I said through the connector as I dug the fangs out of my calf.

"*We're taking major damage here, Chief,*" answered Felicia. "*I'm going to have to get into werewolf mode.*"

*"I wouldn't do that,"* Chuck warned. *"They'll all turn on you in an instant and you'll die."*

And that's exactly what would happen, which gave me the idea to force myself to go full wolf…assuming I could, anyway.

Rachel wouldn't like it, but after all her fawning and swooning shit, I could deal with that. Besides, if I took the brunt of the damage, that would allow my team to survive this rout. Sometimes a chief's gotta do what a chief's gotta do.

*"Stay in your human form, Felicia,"* I commanded. "I'm *going to go full wolf."*

*"What?"* Rachel blurted. *"Don't do that!"*

*"It's for the best,"* I replied. *"Get ready to hit these guys, please."*

I kicked out at an incoming vampire, hitting him in the jaw. It wouldn't kill him, but it was effective in knocking him out for the time being.

Another one came in, but this time I didn't strike; instead, I caught her hand and spun her around so her back was against my chest. She raked at me with her nails, but I put the pain aside and focused on getting into wolf form.

My mind brought up visions of being up in the hills in the middle of the night. There was a full moon in the sky and the smell of fear was in the air. I was envisioning a hunt. No…wait…that wasn't it. Something else was going on. It was…

I immediately snapped out of it and found that I was dry humping the vampire I'd been holding onto.

"Get off me, you perv," she yelped, and then brought

her foot up behind her, connecting perfectly with my nads.

Clearly, I'd had that coming, but it wasn't like I'd done it on purpose.

As I hit the ground, cradling my bruised berries, I couldn't help but think that the werewolf power flowing through my veins wasn't quite intended for what I thought it was.

## CHAPTER 35

"Stop!" commanded Sylvester from his pulpit. "I believe I shall be the one who gives him the final blow."

I winced and looked up at him. "No offense, pal," I said through gritted teeth, "but I'm not into dudes."

"What?" he replied as a few of the vampires around him chuckled. He glanced at them and then groaned. "You have the mind of a teenager, Officer Dex."

"Thanks," I replied as the pain in my nuts began to subside.

Being a fast healer was sometimes brutal because you tended to feel the pain of healing more severely than the pain of breaking. But since my balls were already aching like a bitch, the reversal wasn't any worse than the original hit.

Regardless, I still had to put on a show. I needed Sylvester to get closer, thinking he was going to be delivering the ultimate knockout punch.

I breathed out and squinted up at him.

"Why'd you bite me in the first place, Sly?" I asked. "If your plan was just to kill me, why didn't you just do that when my back was turned?"

"Because I wanted you to serve under me," he answered. Then he pointed at me irritably. "I don't mean that in a sexual way, either."

"Didn't think you did. Perv."

"I'm not a…" He huffed and gave me a dirty look. "Anyway, it became instantly clear that my venom did not work on you. Thus, it was obvious that you needed to die."

"Makes sense," I panted, staying curled up in the fetal position. "I would've done the same thing."

He appeared shocked by this.

"You would have?"

"Well, I wouldn't have tried to subjugate a bunch of people in the first place, Sly," I pointed out, "but if I *had* done that for whatever reason…say, I was born with an incredibly small penis or something…then, yeah."

"Are you inferring that I have a small member?"

"Inferring?" I answered. "No, Sly. I wouldn't do that. I'm the kind of guy who says it like it is, ya know?"

"Good, because…" He paused and tilted his head and growled. "That's it. I've had about enough of you."

He pulled back his fist and dived directly down to punch me on the side of the head.

Unfortunately for him, I moved.

Punching a person's head can hurt your knuckles something fierce, but hitting concrete is quite a bit worse.

"Ahhh!" Sylvester squealed as he held his limp hand.

"You weren't supposed to move!"

"Oh?" I replied, feigning sorrow. "My bad, Sly. I should have just let you kill me so you wouldn't hurt your hand, eh?"

That's when his fangs came out.

Of course, so did mine.

"*Ian,*" Rachel yelled through the connector, "*we've got djinn incoming.*"

"*What?*" I croaked as Sylvester lunged for my throat. I batted him away. "*Why are they here?*"

"*How the hell should I know?*" she spat.

"*Well, find the fuck out, Rachel!*" I shot back.

I should have expected her response, but I didn't.

It was, "*Oooh.*"

I jumped to my feet just as Sylvester got to his. He obviously knew he was out of his league because the look on his face was one of fear.

"You *are* an uber, right?" I asked as we circled each other. "I mean, you don't really theem like one, but you've been giving powerth and thit to people, tho it'th made me wonder."

"Of course I'm an uber." He pointed at his fangs. "Venom."

"That'th it?"

"Yes. Why are you lisping?"

"Oh," I said, rolling my eyes. "I haven't gotten uthed to thpeaking with my teeth out yct."

He nodded understandingly. "Ah, yes. It takes awhile. The main thing is to control your tongue. You have to pull it back a little when you speak."

"Yeah?" I moved my tongue a couple of times.

"Thankth for the tip."

"No problem."

He lurched forward, but I snapped out a jab that caught him right in the nose. That type of hit would usually draw blood, but seeing that he was a vampire, not much happened aside from a whistling that sounded with each breath.

"*The djinn are touching all of the vampires,*" Rachel informed me.

"*What, like, inappropriately?*"

"*No, you idiot,*" she replied. I can't believe I actually missed her calling me that. "*I'm saying that they're knocking them all out.*"

"*Oh, that's good.*"

Sylvester tried to lunge at me again.

I punched him again in response.

This time I connected with his eye. Now he was whistling and winking. It looked rather humorous, from my perspective, but his face held a visage of fury.

"Damn it!" he yelled at his minions. "Hold him so I can kill him."

But it was already too late.

The djinn had been funneling through the crowd and vampires were dropping like flies. Or was it dropping like bats? They didn't really turn into bats or anything, but... well, never mind.

I took a step forward and faked a punch at Sylvester. Once he brought up his hands to block, I full-on soccer kicked him in his cajones.

He fell over and began to whimper.

"Doethn't feel tho great, doeth it?" I taunted him and

then I pulled my fangs back in. "I mean, I know *you* didn't kick me in the danglers, but one of your subjects did, so turn around is fair play."

One of the djinn started to reach for Sylvester.

"No," I warned, pointing at her. "Don't touch him. He's an uber. It could kill you."

It was Elaine.

Her face went red with anger, but she backed away.

"Didn't I tell you to stay out of this?" I snapped at her. "We had everything under control."

"On the contrary," she argued. "When we walked in you were on the ground about to be killed, and the rest of your officers were already damn near overrun. You wouldn't have lasted another minute had we not shown up to save your asses."

She had me there. The fact was that I probably could have gone into a rage and started killing everyone with magical mayhem, but the majority of these vampires didn't deserve that. Just like the sentry dude who had tried to help Elaine when he'd thought she'd hurt herself in a fall.

"Fair enough," I acquiesced. "Still, what if your people had been hurt?"

She scanned the area. "A few of them were, in fact. But they all knew what they were getting into."

"Can you cure them all, by chance?" Chuck asked Elaine as my crew walked over. He pointed at Sylvester, who was still busily clutching his marbles. "They were all poisoned by him."

Elaine nodded and the djinn who were still standing closed their eyes and began whispering something I couldn't understand. It wasn't as bad as the wizard's pygmy chants when they ran spells, but it was still odd sounding.

Like a bunch of zombies, all the vampires stood back up. Well, all of them except for Sylvester, of course.

After a few moments, Elaine and the rest of the djinn heaved and opened their eyes in shock. I grabbed her before she fell over, but many of her underlings hit the ground. Obviously, Sylvester's poison ran deeper than just blood.

"Are you okay?" I asked, to which Elaine nodded as she blinked a few times. "I'm guessing you *can't* cure them?"

She shook her head. Her face and coloring told me I was about to have fresh puke on my shoes. I turned her at the last second and she horked all over Sylvester.

"That's disgusting," he railed, but he still maintained his fetal position.

The doors kicked open a second later and in came Serena and Warren. They were both holding what looked like automatic weapons.

"Get down, Chief," yelled Warren. "We've got this."

"No!" yelled Chuck as my wizard and forensics expert began firing.

Griff launched himself at Chuck, knocking his partner to the ground as the rest of us, djinn included, all hit the deck.

"*Stop!*" I commanded through the connector at Serena. "*Stop firing right now!*"

She did.

But it was too late.

All of the vampires were down.

## CHAPTER 36

"What have you done?" Chuck stammered, staring at the fallen bodies. "They're your own people, Serena!"

Before she could respond, a few of the vampires began moving around.

"What happened?" said one of them.

"Where am I?" said another.

Within thirty seconds, they were all awake and looking around like a bunch of people who had just roused from a night of heavy drinking.

I tilted my head at my two gun-wielding agents. "Serena?"

She walked over and set down the gun. Then she took out a small, pellet-sized projectile from her pocket, and handed it over to me. It looked kind of like a BB, but it was red instead of copper.

"When we got back to the shop," she explained, "Warren and I immediately started working on the blood we'd taken from the werebear and the werewolf. Using Warren's magic and my healing capabilities, we were able to synthesize an anti-venom." She took a breath. "Then we brought in Turbo and got him working. Fortunately, he had already been developing these little pellets, so it was somewhat serendipitous that he had them ready to test just as we needed them."

"Nice," I said, smiling big. "So, everyone here is cured, then?"

"They should be," she answered.

Chuck, clearly unable to contain himself, reached out and gave both Serena and Warren a big hug.

"Any permanent damage to your guys?" I asked Elaine. "It appears we have a cure, if so."

"No, no," she answered with a wave of her hand. "We were just mentally blocked by the vampires. A block like that feels like you've smacked your head against a brick wall. We'll be fine."

"Great." I took a deep breath and put my hands on my hips. "Well, it looks like this little fiasco is over."

And that's when Sylvester did something I didn't realize he was capable of.

He made some weird sign with his free hand—the other was holding his damaged junk.

A blue light surrounded him almost instantly.

Then he disappeared.

But not before grabbing my leg.

Meaning, I ended up going with him.

# CHAPTER 37

My vision was blurred when I came to. I tried to shake it, but it took a lot of effort. When I went to rub my eyes, I found that I was tightly chained in the shape of an X.

"What the shit is going on?" I mumbled, each word resulting in a pounding sensation in my head. "Did you do this to me, Sly?"

In response, I felt the sting of a very hard slap across my cheek.

"Don't call me that name again," Sylvester warned.

"Damn. Sorry, Sly…erm, Sylvester." I then spit out some blood and waited for my head to stop buzzing. "Where are we?"

"In my lair."

"Well, that's ominous."

"You will either turn here or you will die, Officer Dex." His voice was laced with a venom that was even nastier than the kind he passed to his victims. "You will be mine."

"I already told you that I'm not into dudes, Sly."

He slapped me again.

I spit again.

"You're really going to have to quit hitting, dude."

"Or what?"

Even though I felt pretty dizzy, I replied with, "Or I'll have to kill you."

He sniffed at that and I saw the blurred image of him walking away.

My eyes didn't sting or anything, but it sure felt like there was some type of gel on them. I slammed my eyelids shut and moved my eyes back and forth rapidly, trying to loosen whatever it was that had been stopping me from seeing clearly.

It didn't work.

"Could you at least tell me what's in my eyes?"

He giggled like a deranged person.

"I shot my venom all over you."

"That sounds dirty, Sly," I pointed out, then I flinched. "Wait, you *do* literally mean venom, right? You didn't tug your banana on me while I was out, did you?"

There was a delay in his response.

"Oh, shit," I said, feeling disgusted. "I can't believe you, man! You don't go whipping off on a dude while—"

"Officer Dex," he interrupted with a bark, "I did *not* do any such thing. Just because you are a juvenile-minded twit, does not mean everyone is."

I sighed with relief.

"Thank goodness." I laughed a bit. "I gotta tell ya, Sly, I was about to puke right then."

"You're a very sick man, Officer Dex."

"Says the guy who squirted his venom all over me," I remarked.

I tried pulling against the chains, but they were too tight. I could barely even move an inch. Not being able to see didn't help matters either. It was a bit odd that the venom wasn't stinging my eyes, though. I would have imagined it would be quite stingy indeed.

"So what's the plan?" I asked.

"I've already told you, Officer Dex."

"Yeah, yeah, yeah," I droned in response. "You'll either turn me gay or kill me."

"What?" he hissed. "No. I did *not* say I was going to try and turn you gay…" I heard his foot tapping. "You're trying to get a rise out of me again."

I chuckled at his phrasing.

"Honestly, you are a child."

"Better than being an adult," I said with a grin, looking in the general direction of his voice. "In all seriousness, though, I'm going to have to kill you now."

"And how do you propose to accomplish that?"

"Magic."

"Ah, right. Magic. Why hadn't I thought of that?"

That was the problem. He hadn't. His sarcastic tone made that abundantly clear.

I turned my attention inward, unleashing a vent of energy that I channeled into my bloodstream. It *was* magic and I was controlling it. Gone were the days of only being able to cast little light spells. I was now directing and manipulating the fabric of power to suit my needs, and my current need was to clear my eyes.

Okay, so doing that *did* sting.

JOHN P. LOGSDON & CHRISTOPHER P. YOUNG

But I merely clenched my teeth until the pain subsided.

I slowly opened my eyes and found everything was clear again. That was pretty incredible since I didn't even know I could...

Wait a second. If I could clear the venom from my eyes, shouldn't I also be able to clear it from the rest of my body?

It was worth a shot.

"Officer Dex," Sylvester spoke up, interrupting my desire to attempt ridding myself of his venom, "I believe that you are now under my control, yes?"

"Uh..." If I said I was, he might unchain me. "Let me check. Yep. I totally am."

"Hmmm." He placed his hands on his little metal desk. It looked kind of like a metal table that you put your dog on at the vet. "Ah well. I suppose I will just have to run this little show without you."

"No, seriously, Sly...erm, Sylvester. I'm totally under your control."

He lifted up a long knife from the metal desk and began walking toward me.

Now, just so you know, I wasn't a fan of knives. I'd been punched, kicked, shot, given a wedgie, and even had my head dunked in a toilet (long story), and all of them sucked, but being stabbed was the worst.

"All right, boss," I said, as the energy began to build up in my veins again. "What say we put the knife down, eh? No reason to go stabbing people. It's not nice."

"You may have noticed, Officer Dex, that I have little desire to be nice." He ran the dull side of the blade across my neck. "It's such a shame to have to spill your blood. You have incredible potential." He shrugged and frowned. "Alas, it is what it is."

He pulled the knife back and smiled sinisterly.

"Nope," I stated as the power that had been welling up unleashed through my eyes like a couple of suns.

Smoldering had nothing on this shit.

Sylvester dropped the knife and flew backwards as if he'd been hit by a tsunami. He crashed against the table, bending at an odd angle in the process before collapsing to the floor.

I quickly channeled the energy pouring from my eyes into my wrists and ankles instead. It resulted in shattering the cuffs that held me in place. Then I stepped away from the X and walked over to the uber vampire. A gentle kick told me he was still unconscious.

Good.

It was about time I had my hands on one of these uber pricks.

"Well, that sounded wrong," I said to the room.

## CHAPTER 38

*J*'d attempted using my magic to clear the venom from my system, but it didn't work. Worse, every time I tried, I blacked out.

Obviously that was some strong venom.

When Sylvester regained consciousness, he opened his eyes to see me sitting in front of him. I'd put his ass up on the X just like he'd done to me originally. Unfortunately, I'd blown apart the cuffs, but I'd found some rope and tied him up nicely.

Evil overlord-wannabes almost always had rope lying around.

"What happened?" he slurred.

"The tables have turned," I explained. "I have shot my venom on you this time."

His eyes snapped open at that. "What?"

"I'm joking, Sly," I said with a laugh. "Only a dude with a one-inch dick would do something like that, you know?"

JOHN P. LOGSDON & CHRISTOPHER P. YOUNG

"Oh, good…. Wait, what?"

I got off the chair that I'd pulled over and started walking around the X. He struggled against the binds, but it was abundantly clear that he didn't have the power I possessed. Still, I couldn't blame the guy for trying.

"Now, here's how it's going to go, Sly," I said, flashing the very knife he had planned to do me in with. "You're going to tell me what I want to know. In exchange, I won't kill you."

"You won't?" he asked hopefully.

I gave him a serious look. "You have my word, Sly." I raised an eyebrow at him. "I *will* send you on a long vacation to a five-by-four room with bunkbeds and a guy name Al who will probably want to play a game of poke-the-bottom with you, but that's better than dying." I rubbed my chin. "I guess." Then I shrugged as if it didn't really matter to me. "Anyway, my first question is how you transferred us to your lair?"

"Oh, that's easy," he replied, acting like Mr. Helpful all of a sudden. "I had the goblin mage infuse me with the ability." He grunted. "Took him forever, let me tell you. Apparently, things like that are better suited for wizards."

"Yep." I paced in front of him. "All right, so how is it that you have been able to give extra powers to everyone you've bitten?"

He winced, looking suddenly uncomfortable.

"It's…part…of…my…venom." Each word was said with effort. "It…enhances…things."

So that meant it was similar to whatever happened to PPD officers when they got their upgrades, but better. Well, depending on your perspective, anyway. PPD officers weren't enslaved by the department, even if it felt like it sometimes.

"Where's the wizard chick who helped you talk with Spunx?"

"Spunx?"

"I meant Spanx," I clarified. "I'm talking about the goblin you contacted from the Netherworld and sent off to New York-New York for a little fun."

"Ah," he said, nodding. "Kaitlin Fezzmul. She was a goody two-shoes, actually. Didn't...want to help me out, but it's...amazing what you can get people to do when..." He groaned, apparently feeling more anguish over having to spill his guts. Once his discomfort cleared, he smirked like an evil piece of cock bologna and looked up at me. "I had to kill her. Couldn't leave a trail, you know? Her screams were so...pleasing."

I stopped pacing.

"You're a foreskin pimple, you know that, Sly?" I said rhetorically, wanting to slap him.

So I did.

He yelped.

"Now,"—I got in close and snarled at him—"you must have knowledge about the ubers, and I want to know what you know right the fuck now."

His face turned red and he scrunched his eyes. The look of discomfort from before was nothing compared to how he appeared now. Sylvester had the look of a man who had been struck with a severe migraine.

"What's the matter, Sly?"

"My head," he moaned. "What...are you doing...to me?"

"I'm not doing anything to you," I replied. "I just want to know what you know about the other ubernaturals. Tell me and things go easier on you with the Tribunal."

"Okay," he cried in anguish. His breathing was shallow and rapid. "We…were…all…part…of an…" His breath caught and his eyes snapped open. They were completely black, and they were bulging. "No! No! Ahhh!"

And that's when I got covered in brain goop.

## CHAPTER 39

The Directors arrived a few minutes after I did. They were usually already there when I walked in, so this was a little strange. But they'd been a bit odd ever since the ubers started invading the Strip.

After about five minutes, they finally arrived.

"We're sorry to have kept you waiting, Mr. Dex," said O.

"Why are you apologizing to him?" asked Silver. "He works for us."

"Because it's common courtesy, Silver."

Silver seemed on edge, which made sense seeing that it was a vampire uber we had dealt with this time.

"Tell us what happened, Mr. Dex," he demanded.

I detailed a carefully worded version of the story to him, including how the djinn helped to neutralize the vampires, and how Elaine Kouross and her crew should be honored. I also discussed how Serena, Warren, and Turbo had worked together to cure the vampires who were infected and enslaved. I left the parts out regarding the changes to my person, though, especially knowing that EQK was suspicious of me already.

"Did you get his name?" Silver asked.

"Sylvester Melbourne."

Another round of silence.

It was almost humorous at this point. Whenever I named the last few ubers, these guys went quiet and then they started griping at each other before they abruptly left the meeting.

This time I was going to try a different tactic.

"Anyway," I started, "I wanted to apologize to EQGay for not being more direct with him last time we met."

"Huh?" replied EQK, not bothered by my using a derivative version of his name.

"At our last meeting," I clarified. "I was not feeling well and so I didn't treat you with the proper respect."

"You feeling okay, Wrong-Sex Dex?" EQK asked, sounding baffled.

"Better now, you winged butt plug."

"Good, good."

I sensed that O wanted to chastise me for calling EQK a name, but he had no legs to stand on. I'd claimed that it was part of my one-person culture to call people names. What could he say?

"So," Silver began, sounding like he knew I was up to something, "you're not going to question us about Sylvester Melbourne?"

"No, sir," I replied. "I understand that you can't share information, so there's really no point in my pressing the issue."

"I see," he replied dubiously. Then he added, "Actually, no I don't. You've been complaining like a school child for the last number of meetings, and now you've suddenly just accepted your fate?"

"He said he has, you fanged knob thumper," EQK blurted, coming to my defense, exactly as I was hoping he would.

"Excuse me?" Silver said at length.

"You're excused," EQK replied. "Don't worry about him, Dexnose, he's just angry because his wife found out he fucks goats."

"I…what?"

I couldn't see any of them, of course, but I could imagine the three older dudes on my left side of the podium staring incredulously at the pixie on the right. It was all I could do not to laugh.

"Wait a second, Fang Face," said EQK, "are you telling me you *didn't* tell your wife you fuck goats?"

"Of course I didn't!"

"Ahhh, probably wise," mused EQK. "She may not understand, after all. Yep, that's a smart move all around, I'd say."

There was a moment of silence.

"You are merely trying to get a rise out of me, EQK," Silver grated.

"Like the goats do, you mean?"

"I do *not* have relations with goats!"

"Finally moved on to sheep, eh?" EQK replied. I had to cover my mouth because the smiling could not be stopped. "Goats *do* seem a little unrefined for you, to be honest, but I just thought you were into sexually slumming it."

"You're a fool," Silver hissed.

"By the way," EQK said like a friend giving advice, "you may want to wash thoroughly after you bone livestock, you fiendish fanged one. I hear that werewolves can smell sheep ass on your dick." After a quick pause, he added, "Just ask Zack, he sniffs dicks all the time."

"What?" yelped Zack.

That's when the sound of a hand slammed on the top of a desk. It came from the center of the room, meaning it was O.

"Enough!" he bellowed. "This lack of professionalism is ridiculous. I don't care what your personal cultural norms are, EQK, if you don't respect those on this board I will request your removal."

"All right, all right," EQK boomed in response. "Sheesh! You act like it's *my* fault that Silver fucks sheep and Zack sniffs dicks!"

I laughed.

Sometimes you just can't help it. It took me about a minute to regain control. Finally, I climbed back into my chair and wiped my eyes.

"Are you through, Mr. Dex?" asked O in a dark tone.

"Yes, sir," I replied, fighting the laughter. "Sorry."

O sighed heavily. "Is there anything else you need from us today?"

Here was my shot. Griping, moaning, and complaining at them about general details hadn't worked. I was hoping that a direct question regarding a facet of an uber's powers might.

"I was wondering if any of you might know how Mr.

Melbourne's venom was able to increase powers for supernaturals?"

"He was genetically tweaked," EQK answered.

"EQK!" Zack bellowed.

"Zack!" mocked EQK in response.

"You're out of control."

"Says the guy who pees on fire hydrants."

They started bickering back and forth, but I'd tuned them out. My plan had worked. Getting EQK on my side caused him to respond as he would to a peer. So these ubers were genetically altered also?

"Excuse me," I yelled above the din, silencing them. "Are the ubers all past cops?"

"That's enough for today," O said before anyone could answer me.

Three of the lights went out.

O's remained.

"I'm not happy with what you've just done, Mr. Dex," he said evenly.

"And what is that, exactly?"

"You manipulated this panel to get information that you knew was classified," he replied. "I will be placing a formal reprimand on your record."

I nodded. "So does that mean they *were* past cops?"

"Good day, Mr. Dex."

# CHAPTER 40

The Three Angry Wives Pub wasn't exactly teeming with action. Seeing that it was a Wednesday, I wasn't surprised. Hump day was often slow for most places on the outskirts of town.

I snagged a booth and ordered a Rusty Nail.

It was usually about now that Gabe walked through the door, gave me some advice, slipped me one of his fancy *Words*, and then bolted before answering any of my questions.

But this time, he didn't.

An hour passed and he was still nowhere to be seen.

I ordered some wings and tore through them. After the day I'd had, I needed some serious grub. I still wanted that Big Ass Burrito from Tommy Rocker's, but Gabe didn't frequent that place. Besides, it was tradition to show up here whenever I finished a case. I wasn't one who subscribed to superstition, but I did believe in patterns.

Gabe, apparently, felt differently.

Three hours in, it was clear that Gabe wasn't going to show. I don't know why, but I kind of felt that I should have expected it. Apparently, when he said he was out of *Words* for me, that was code for "Bye-bye, Ian."

It kind of bummed me out, to be honest. There was something nice about having someone outside of the PPD to talk to about stuff, even if it was only for a few minutes at a shot. Yeah, there was always Dr. Vernon, but it just wasn't the same.

I paid the check and walked to the door, giving one final scan around the room.

"Right," I said as I pushed out into the night.

## CHAPTER 41

"So he never showed up?" Rachel asked as I stared down at her back. "That's odd."

"Very," I agreed, "but can we *not* talk about Gabe right now?"

She was tied to the bed, facedown, and I was wearing a mask and holding a whip. It felt odd for me to be in this position. It was a role-reversal, after all.

"Sorry," she said.

"Right." I cleared my throat. "Okay, so before we begin, I'll need your safe word."

She wiggled her tushy and giggled.

"What's funny?" I asked, confused.

"I've just never had to give a safe word before. It's kind of exciting."

"Ah."

"How about we go with 'harder, faster, don't stop'?"

"Very funny," I grunted. "You need to take this seriously, Rachel, or you may get hurt."

"Isn't that the point?"

"Well, yes, but I don't want you to be seriously injured."

"All right, all right," she replied with a sigh. "I'll go with 'fucksnacks'."

I rolled my eyes and lowered my head. Sometimes she was such a pain. It was as though she were trying to irk me, which I guess made sense under these circumstances.

"You may remember that you say 'fucksnacks' all the time when we're having sex, Rachel."

Her head turned slightly. "I do?"

"Right before you orgasm," I answered. "I've always found that odd…" I coughed. "Erm…I mean interesting, to be honest."

"Huh. I guess I'm always so wrapped up in the moment that I never realized it."

"Probably." I was starting to lose my interest, not that I had a lot of desire in this direction in the first place. It was still exceedingly odd that she wanted me to dominate her. This just wasn't our normal dynamic. "How about choosing something that is completely nonsexual?"

"You mean like 'Warren'?" she giggled again.

I sighed.

"Sorry," she laughed. "Okay, okay. Uh…I'll say 'chandelier'."

"Perfect."

Surprisingly, The Admiral had been rather tight-lipped during this entire exchange. He *was* a bit preoccupied, though.

I'd also managed to avoid the valkyrie conversation by sternly saying, "Not now" when Rachel brought up the topic. My firmness is what landed me in the position of wearing a mask, holding a whip, and standing behind my tied-up girlfriend while asking her for a safe word.

With a light sigh, I pulled back the whip and admired her perfect bottom. It was such a shame to have to redden it as I was about to do, but the key to a successful relationship was supporting each other's needs.

Still, I wanted to take it slow.

Rachel may have been excited by the prospect of this, but she'd never been on the receiving end of this style of play before.

And, so, with a somewhat gentle flick of my wrist, the whip snapped out and struck her left butt cheek.

"Chandelier!"

## Thanks for Reading

If you enjoyed this book, would you please leave a review at the site you purchased it from? It doesn't have to be a book report... just a line or two would be fantastic and it would really help us out!

## John P. Logsdon
www.JohnPLogsdon.com

John was raised in the MD/VA/DC area. Growing up, John had a steady interest in writing stories, playing music, and tinkering with computers. He spent over 20 years working in the video games industry where he acted as designer and producer on many online games. He's written science fiction, fantasy, humor, and even books on game development. While he enjoys writing lighthearted adventures and wacky comedies most, he can't seem to turn down writing darker fiction. John lives with his wife, son, and Chihuahua.

## Christopher P. Young

Chris grew up in the Maryland suburbs. He spent the majority of his childhood reading and writing science fiction and learning the craft of storytelling. He worked as a designer and producer in the video games industry for a number of years as well as working in technology and admin services. He enjoys writing both serious and comedic science fiction and fantasy. Chris lives with his wife and an ever-growing population of critters.

CRIMSON MYTH PRESS

*Crimson Myth Press* offers more books by this author as well as books from a few other hand-picked authors. From science fiction & fantasy to adventure & mystery, we bring the best stories for adults and kids alike.

www.CrimsonMyth.com